Alix in Academe

Alix in Academe

Jeanne Purdy

CREATIVE ARTS BOOK COMPANY
Berkeley, CA 2000

Special thanks to Dwight Purdy, for writing the poems and songs. And to Rose Marie Abbott, Vicky Demos, Fred Peterson, and Katherine Gonier, for all their help.

Alix in Academe

Chapter One

Alix Attends the Assembly
and is Bored to Sleep

Alix and her mother Eleanor had been touring campuses, trying to choose the one Alix would attend. This was the sixth, and they hoped the last. It was a beautiful campus, located in a former agricultural college, and indeed, the remnants of its former self were visible. A hen-house, a dovecote, a barn, rabbit hutches, a small turkey barn, and a three-story structure labeled House of Fowls surrounded the campus, which also contained a large duck pond filled with ducks, geese, swans, and muskrat mounds. The home for the animal supervisor was still used, now by an assistant dean who functioned as the dean of women had functioned in former days, and as a general assistant to the 'real' dean. The assistant was generally called the Baby Dean, but not to her face.

The weather was cool for June, so cool that Alix was wearing her usual assortment of sentimental shirts, sweat-shirts, and jeans. She wore the T-shirt given her by her father, complete with his company logo, sort of, on the front: SPAM. He worked as a technical engineer at the Hor-mel Plant. She wore her boyfriend Tim's high school wres-tling sweatshirt with the school name on the front and his on the back, and her own high school honor society wind-breaker with her name on the front and the school name on the back. She also wore the fisherman's hat Eleanor had given her, embroidered with daisies and sunflowers by Eleanor and Alix's younger sister Lily. Alix always tried to wear something given her by each family mem-ber, partly to flatter each, partly to feel secure. Eleanor had been Alix's mother for eight years, since Alix was ten years old. Alix's own mother had died when Alix was eight and Lily was four, and Alix no longer remembered her except as a shadow.

Eleanor's first gift to Alix was a copy of *Alice in Won-derland*, and it had caused Alix to fall in love with the book, with fantasy, and with Eleanor. Alix had used the book of-ten, writing a book report on it every time one was as-signed throughout junior high and high school. She had named her cats Dinah and Cheshire after the real and the fantasy cats in *Alice*. In her backpack was the same old copy of *Alice* and Alix's favorite stuffed animal Puppy, her first Christmas present from Eleanor. Puppy went every-where with Alix, and she often joked about writing a series of children's books—*Puppy Goes to Camp, Puppy Learns to Sail, Puppy Rides a Horse*—to parallel her own experiences. Alix hoped to extend Puppy's adventures as she published, and future books would include foreign travel, *Puppy Tours the Pyramids, Puppy Visits the Vatican, Puppy Climbs the Alps*, when Alix could afford travel. Alix thought often that a life of writing books while living and teaching at a rural college, such as Lewis Carroll's, sounded ideal. She hoped to start a writing career even before she finished a BA in Creative Writing.

Alix settled into her seat at the assembly for visiting students, all prospective students for the fall term. Eleanor sat beside her, taking notes and whispering comments to Alix as the president described the student body. 'We have the *best* dormitories. Each has a gym and a jacuzzi, and each floor has a recreation room with TVs and VCRs.

'We have the *best food*: vegetarian meals, Chinese meals, pizza, plus all kinds of Italian dishes—spaghetti, lasagna —did I mention different kinds of pizza?'

Alix noticed his round body and small head and smaller hat. He resembled a flightless bird, not a dodo, more like—it couldn't be an ostrich, could it?

Then the president began introducing others: distinguished guests, vice presidents, assistant vice presidents, assistant dean, acting assistant dean, directors, the acting assistant director . . . Alix's attention drifted and she dozed until she heard the President saying, 'And now my time is up.' And she awoke as he introduced the dean.

Alix saw a large woman wearing an even larger dress, bright red, shapeless, falling in loose folds around her and swirling as she walked to the podium. Several gold necklaces glittered and clinked as she walked. The dean proved to be even more enthusiastic about the institution. 'We have *won*derful relationships between faculty and students, making this a *won*derful community.

'We have *won*derful classes, a *won*derful curriculum.'

Eleanor whispered to Alix, 'What makes them *wonder*ful? I wish she'd be more specific. The other colleges gave us specific descriptions.'

Two faculty members sitting behind Alix and Eleanor began expressing their doubts about the dean's 'wonderful' assessment. 'She doesn't even teach. She wouldn't know a wonderful class from a wake.'

The other faculty member said, 'She's the chair of the curriculum committee, so of course she says the curriculum is wonderful. But saying it's so doesn't make it so. She doesn't know a wonderful curriculum from a Wonderbra.'

The dean continued, breathing more deeply as she described the courses and policies. 'We have a *won*derful policy forbidding any kind of harassment by speech. We forbid the use of epithets, slurs, or negative stereotyping on the grounds of race, color, national or ethnic origin, gender, sexual orientation, age, weight, religion, marital status, veteran status, or disability. We also forbid insults regarding citizenship, culture, HIV status, political affiliation or belief, or pregnancy status.'

Eleanor and Alix looked at each other. 'How can they enforce this?' asked Eleanor.

'Who reports violations?' asked Alix.

Their questions were immediately addressed by the dean: 'To enforce this policy is a *won*derful apparatus of boards and panels. Volunteer advocates have been trained to represent complainants and defendants. I have set up workshops to provide mandatory harassment education for all faculty, students, and staff.'

'What about administrators?' asked Eleanor. 'What about enforcement? Who investigates? Who does the investigator report to? Some campuses cover up these things by having only internal investigations. That's what happened at my alma mater. Nothing was ever resolved to the victims' satisfaction.'

The dean inhaled, visibly changing her shape as the folds of her dress rearranged about her. 'We have a *won*derful course for all our new students, with a *won*derful syllabus. Each class is only twelve students, and only the best professors teach it. Students learn to express themselves because every class period is totally devoted to ex-

pressing ideas and opinions. Students discuss timely top-
ics. All the professors love this course because it is the
most humane course we teach. Every one of you will love
it just as much. It deals with the only issues that really
count:' (Here she reached into her pocket for a list of the
important issues—and read them while trying not to let
everyone see that she was reading from a list.) 'Freedom.
Autonomy. Fairness. Love. This is what you will learn
from this course, and you will agree with everyone who
has taken The Course that it teaches all this and more.'

Many of the faculty seated behind her nodded at each
of these sentences. One of the faculty members seated
behind Alix and Eleanor said, 'Yeah, right. That was an
excellent blend of half-truths, near-truths, and blatant
falsehoods.'

'Freedom? Autonomy? Fairness? Love? How about
Obedience! Deceit! Avarice! And Manipulation! Those will
help you succeed with the dean,' replied the other faculty
member.

'The party line,' agreed the first faculty. 'Anyone who
wants to get ahead has to pretend to love The Course. Then
the dean gives out grants, paid leaves, and travel money
as a reward.'

'When did freedom or autonomy ever help any faculty
here? Scholarship might be praised, but it isn't rewarded.
The best scholarship or best teaching means little to her
unless she's decided to promote that faculty. If she has,
then the scholarship and teaching are the reasons. Oth-
erwise, forget it,' commented the second speaker. Alix
glanced around and saw two small men with light brown
hair, similar faces, and glasses. She could hardly tell them
apart.

'The very best people go unrecognized year after year
because they don't cooperate,' said one sandy-haired man.

Alix was becoming bored by the dean's speech, but
her interest revived with the next statement. 'We are com-

pletely on-line. Not only do we have computers for each student, but the faculty also have them. Each has been assigned a computer, and they have all learned to communicate by E-mail, so that faculty and students are in constant communication, twenty-four hours a day. When faculty leave campus, they have laptops so students can always communicate with them. Communication builds community!'

Alix perked up at this news and smiled at Eleanor. She would be able to remain in constant touch with her boyfriend Tim.

The dean began introducing faculty, beginning with the new members, who were all sitting together. They smiled, stood, and waved at the same time. 'wonderful additions to our faculty. Welcome aboard.'

Alix noticed the older faculty in a group behind the new members. They seemed haggard. Some were nervous. The dean read names from a list, then announced, 'These members have just received tenure.' The group smiled, stood, and waved.

Then the Dean introduced a vice president who took out the Institutional Data Book—dozens of charts on transparencies—and began going through some essential statistics about students, class sizes, class loads, numbers of majors in each department, and Alix tuned out. She found almost all numbers too boring to listen to, and these were worse than boring.

Next came another vice president, whose speech was so vague that Alix gave up on it midway. He began with the usual 'Universities are about excellence. The abstraction is apt, but such universal evocations of quality need interpretation that they not become shibboleth savants. Particular clarification is required as our institution asserts its transcendent concern with one dimension of academic excellence: the educational dimension as applied to the capable and achievement-oriented undergraduate student.

Specifically, we are in the business of providing challenging educational opportunities for qualified students who seek both breadth and depth in their collegiate studies.' No one could listen to this for very long, and Alix certainly couldn't. She closed her eyes for a few minutes. Then she tried again to listen but nodded off until she felt Eleanor sit up straighter.

Eleanor was looking at the door as two faculty members entered late. One of the two faculty members behind Alix glanced at them and said, 'Speak of the devils. Both of these two support the dean by praising The Course. They both will do anything to gain her approval, even if it means losing all self-respect.' The first latecomer, with a round chest and short legs, sat down immediately. The second person moved his heavy briefcase from one hand to another and used his free hand to tap the shoulders of people he wanted to stand for him so he could step over them and reach the center of the row. He had a long scrawny neck and pouches under his eyes and chin. 'Turkey,' said Alix and Eleanor together. He certainly did not regard himself as a turkey, for he preened more like a peacock as he opened his briefcase and spread out his papers. He wanted to correct a statement made about him at the last assembly, and he had brought his own transparency describing the mistake and offering his new corrected version. He took the transparency to the projector but it didn't fit until he arranged it diagonally, and then everyone in the assembly had to tilt their heads to read it. His head seemed permanently tilted to the right.

'A student orientation isn't the place for corrections,' Alix heard the faculty member behind her say.

'What an ego!' commented the other. 'Like we care about what someone said about him three months ago!'

'Turkey!' said the first.

The last late faculty member came in as the dean once again listed various members of the administration, omitting the names because titles were more important to her: assistant dean, director, acting assistant dean, assistant director, acting assistant director . . . department chair . . . acting assistant chair . . . acting assistant . . . alligator . . . dodo . . . turkey . . . Alix's head tilted onto Eleanor's shoulder just as the late faculty member crept toward the seat next to her. Twitching hands and nose reminded Alix of a rabbit, a rabbit in a big hurry, a rabbit with a lot on his mind, a mind that couldn't hold a lot.

The latecomer sat next to her, muttering, *'Quelle heure est'il?'*

Chapter Two

Down the Chute into Virtual Reality

Alix blinks and looks around. She's no longer in the assembly, among people, but in some kind of meeting hall, among large birds. The hall is decorated with plants, Native American prints, and welcome signs. The large birds are speaking in the voices she's just heard in the assembly. The two voices speaking near her sound like the president and vice president, but she sees an ostrich and a parrot.

Alix wonders if she's now in virtual reality because she sees a large bird with a small head—could it be an ostrich?—speaking with an equally large parrot with a yellow bill and blue body. Alix recognizes the ostrich as the president of the institution. Ostrich is explaining the financial state of the institution. 'The institution is in deep, yes,

I said deep—I mean deep—you'd better believe it, deep, debt.'

The voices are coming from a sunken area that looks like a lounge, for it is furnished with couches and a fireplace. As Alix peeps down at the ostrich and parrot, Parrot calls up to her, 'This is a conversation pit. It's from the days when people thought they knew what they were talking about. I'm sorry, I don't recall your name.' Parrot has long blue wings dragging on the floor behind him. Alix realizes that he is the vice president, that his long blue suit is now long blue feathers.

As Alix climbs down into the conversation pit to respond, Ostrich assumes it is *his* name that Parrot does not recall. 'You don't know how relieved I am to hear you say that! I can't remember your name either!' Looking relieved to find that someone else is as forgetful as he is, Ostrich waves his wings.

'Parrot,' says the parrot. 'I am Vice President Parrot. On the one hand, and there is no doubt about it, this is a make-work, dead-end job, but, on the other hand, it's also a vice presidency.'

'We all have a part to play in life,' says Ostrich, 'and your part is being a yes-man. There are lousier parts. I've been looking for you. It's time for you to be evaluated. Give me a list of your duties and I'll give them to the evaluation committee. Also, tell me how well you've done each one.'

'How long will this review take? I have reservations on a flight this weekend.' Parrot looks anxious at the thought of missing a trip.

'No problem,' says Ostrich. 'The committee will be appointed today, review your work tomorrow, and by the day after I can approve the review and reappoint you.' Alix remembers the conversations she heard in the assembly, that only the cooperative faculty are rewarded, and she wonders if Parrot is being reappointed because of his abilities or because he cooperates? It seems that his parroting is valued more than his autonomy or fairness.

'Good,' says Parrot, 'I need a break. I've had meetings every day this week. Breakfast, lunch, and dinner meetings. I'm stuffed full.' Parrot *looks* stuffed. Stuffed and stiff and blue, like a Norwegian blue parrot.

Alix thinks it all absurd, but they look so grave she does not dare laugh. She turns at the sound of hissing air. It is a balloon, no, a balloon dressed somewhat like a person, or a person shaped like a balloon—anyway, it is floating and bobbing as it talks to three other creatures. The first creature has two faces pointing in opposite directions. His name matches his face, for it is Janus JekyllHyde. Both faces are engaged in conversation with the balloon, who Alix learns is called Red Dean. Alix recognizes the red dress and gold necklaces she saw the dean wearing, but this figure is much more inflated. The folds of her dress are disappearing as Red Dean speaks, for she inhales deeply for each breath but never seems to lose air. Alix sees two tiny creatures bouncing rapidly near her knees and she isn't sure at first what they are. One has no legs and stands on his tail end; the other has very small legs and perhaps wings. Their voices are familiar, and she recognizes them as the voices of the faculty members who sat behind her at the assembly, the two small men with sandy hair who resembled each other.

As Alix climbs out of the conversation pit, Red Dean is saying to Janus, or at least to his nearer face, 'There are a lot of books not earning their keep around here. Send them off!' She pulls her dress down around her increasing waist.

Janus agrees, 'Books are easily disposed of. Our greater challenge is in disposing of politically incorrect persons.' Janus's other face frowns. Alix is not sure whether it is agreeing with his partner face or disagreeing.

'How about Parrot?' asks Red Dean. 'He reminds me of an animated duck bringing me the news.' Red Dean adjusts her hair, which has slipped sideways as she sways from side to side, talking with one face of Janus or the other. Alix notices that Red Dean tries to speak with only one of Janus' faces at a time, which makes sense, because the faces often say opposite things.

'Our job is not to impose comfort levels; civility and suasion, not rules and regulations, are the way to shape our community,' says Janus's mild face. It is lean, with droopy eyes, the face of Stan Laurel.

Red Dean nods happily, but her hair slips forward and almost covers her face. Then she addresses Janus's other face, the angry one, saying, 'But the flag burners. We must stop the flag burners.'

'Well,' says Janus's peaceful face, 'we will protect people who are sensitive about being male, female, black, white, Asian, young, old, married, unmarried, straight, gay, Catholic, Jewish, evangelical Protestant, or veterans. We're upholding freedom of speech.' Alix notices that when Janus's two faces talk, it is hard to follow his turns of thought. It is also hard to adjust to seeing his two faces swiveling around, although the faces are quite different. One is large, round, and angry, and has a narrow mustache just under the nose, and the other is lean and sleepy-eyed. The round face, considering the lean face to be a hopeless slackard, forces his own face forward most of the time. Suddenly Alix realizes that if the lean face is that of Stan Laurel, the round is Oliver Hardy.

Red Dean reads from a proclamation. 'Speech is offensive if it discriminatorily alters the condition of any of these groups, or any member of one of these groups, enough to make the individual uncomfortable.' She adjusts her hair, pulls down her dress, and assumes a very serious expression.

'Did we use this code to banish Mother Theresa?' asks Janus. The expressions on both faces remain benign, confusing Alix for the moment.

'She was declared insolent. She thought she was more civil than I am.' Red Dean inhales with a little hiss. Alix has just noticed that Red Dean inhales much, exhales seldom. It's no wonder that her waist is expanding, for all of Red Dean expands with each breath, filling more folds of her dress. Soon it flows out in a tent shape from her neck, a bright red glowing tent with necklaces and a head.

'Then you all understand our code regulating harassing speech?' Red Dean asks the group, her dress billowing around her and rising as her voice rises, causing her necklaces to tangle and jangle.

'It would create a totalitarian atmosphere,' says Janus's lean, mild face, 'and we would have to guard our tongues all the time.' He feels for his tongue. His round face sticks its tongue out, which Alix interprets as disagreement. Perhaps he values totalitarianism, as Red Dean does.

Alix sees the two faculty members approaching, but they are so short Red Dean does not see them at first. Suddenly noticing them, Red Dean glares at the one with no legs. 'Guard! Get that tongue!'

'I'm a slug,' says Slug, ' not a tongue.' Slug is the small person standing on end that Alix saw earlier. She remembers his voice as the faculty member seated behind her at the assembly, the one who muttered that Obedience and Manipulation were more necessary than Autonomy and Freedom. No wonder Red Dean wanted his tongue guarded.

'Then get that other tongue!' shouts Red Dean, growing redder and larger.

'I'm a drone, not a tongue,' says Drone. 'See, I have legs.' Alix knows his voice as the other unguarded tongue, the faculty member criticizing The Course during the assembly.

Red Dean glares at Drone, inhales, and says, 'He doesn't use the legs. He must be a tongue. Guard him!' Alix watches Red Dean take a breath, then another, and another, never exhaling, growing bigger and ever bigger. The folds of her dress disappear altogether—she is now shaped like a taut tent. Her skin is more and more transparent as it stretches, and her tent dress creeps up even though she constantly tugs at it to cover her transparency. Before inhaling, she had struggled to remain upright, because without a skeleton she tended to fall flat. Now, however, all puffed up with breath after breath, she bobs with extra air, positively bobs. Instead of grabbing Drone, Janus grabs Red Dean, to keep her from floating away. She is weighed down only by her four heavy gold necklaces and a bejeweled mace she carries to point with. One necklace looks like a small Afghani bag decorated with six different semiprecious stones, another has a Chinese coin surrounded by characters, the third is a chain of African frogs, and the fourth has a Navaho circle of life with blue, yellow, black, and white stones. She actively supports multiculturalism in her daily jewelry and pronouncements.

Alix is startled to see how big Red Dean has become. 'Does she always expand this way?' Red Dean is quite round and seemingly growing as Alix watches her.

'Only when she is full of hot air,' says Drone. 'Sometimes she is small and flat for weeks at a time. Once, the janitor almost swept her away, but she managed to reinflate in time to stop him and fire him.' Drone looks around to see if Red Dean is near enough to hear him.

'Does the hot air come from the weather?' Alix watches as Red Dean becomes airborne.

'She makes it herself,' says Slug. 'Have you ever heard of a fevered imagination?' Both Slug and Drone watch Red Dean fly off.

'Was she always this way?' Alix asks, never having seen anyone so buoyant and so angry at the same time. She decides that being in charge, as Red Dean is, allows her no rest.

'No,' says Slug, 'she grew in the shade. She used to be all stems. But now her stems have shriveled. And her body expands as her power grows.' Slug himself is three inches high, so he stretches up as much as he can. Alix notices that he stands on end, having no feet and not wishing to lie down and present an even lower profile.

'I think,' says Drone, 'the universe expands one day, shrinks the next, then remains static for a week, then begins the whole process all over again.' Drone is as tiny as Slug but flies up at times to increase his visibility. They both have dun-colored hair and Alix wonders how she will ever tell them apart. They have limited presence and limited visibility. Then she sees that Slug wears a tiny fisherman's hat, with teeny lures, tilted toward the back of his head. He's almost lure-sized himself.

Slug agrees, 'Red Dean is similar, but lately she doesn't shrink. Her responsibilities are growing and she needs to breathe more.' Slug breathes deeply and increases his height to three and a half inches. His growth is a result of will power, not hot air, Alix realizes.

'What are her responsibilities?' asks Alix. She can hardly believe she is talking with a Slug and a Drone about a balloon-shaped dean.

'She's the Commander of the Speech Police,' says Drone, 'and has a uniform to prove it. She says someone has to exert order around here.'

'The Speech Code requires boards and panels as enforcers,' adds Slug, shuddering throughout his body. 'She's the enforcer from hell.'

'Does she serve on the boards and panels?' asks Alix, puzzled. She opens her jacket and sets her backpack down.

'Of course not! She directs. She panels panels. She boards boards. She announces her choices; she's a member ex-officio of all committees,' Slug answers. Alix wonders if Slug has ever been named to a board or panel. She doubts it. He's not enough of a team player in Red Dean's estimation, no matter how many books he's published. In her Guide to Institutional Faculty, Alix finds that Slug has published six books and thirty-six articles. He should be one of Red Dean's Points of Bright—distinguished faculty lights—but his name is not listed.

'She sounds like a windbag!' says Alix, looking to see whether Red Dean is close enough to hear her.

'Careful!' Slug says. 'You've violated the Speech Code. You called her a name!' He shudders again and shrinks several centimeters.

Drone adds, 'Red Dean also contributes to faculty morale. She plans races, contests, and games for the faculty. Everyone who wants tenure, promotions, grants, raises, and leaves must compete. Red Dean dispenses the prizes.'

'She's very careful,' says Slug. 'The sad part about being a dictator is that one has so few close friends and those few have to be watched very carefully. Red Dean's constantly busy overseeing everything.' He looks up, and sure enough, Red Dean floats overhead, overseeing everything.

Alix watches someone she hasn't seen before approach. She is not sure what it is. She sees a tall, gaunt figure dressed in black, a long sweater emphasizing its height, long earrings, and a long black cape. Then Alix sees that the cape is in fact wings folded back, and that the person is a woman with a short hairdo, long nose, and piercing eyes. 'Who's that?' Alix asks.

'Don't call her a that, or you'll be in trouble with the Speech Code,' says Drone. 'She's a she, Dragon Lady, Red Dean's designated deanette.'

By now Alix can hear Dragon Lady muttering, 'Go with the flow.'

Chapter Three

Red Dean's Faculty Races

As Dragon Lady approached, Alix heard her saying to herself, 'Go with the flow, my motto was, Go with the flow, but I had no idea the flow would end up here.'

Here was a muddy field. It was a queer-looking party that had assembled for Red Dean's races. Birds with draggled feathers, animals with wet, swirled fur, and assorted bugs, slugs, frogs, and toads have gathered. Alix, speaking familiarly with some creatures she hadn't met yet, wondered if she were dreaming, then asked Slug where she was. 'Is this a virtual reality?'

'No,' said Slug. 'This is a dream.' Slug now expanded into the shape and size of a fire hydrant. His hat expanded with him, fortunately.

'How do you know?' asked Alix, finding it much easier to converse with the expanded Slug.

'Easy,' replied Slug. 'We've shifted into past tense. Virtual reality is present tense.'

This conversation, as well as certain characters she recognized, reminded Alix of Wonderland. She recognized Red Dean as Red Queen, and of course Ostrich and Parrot, and arriving at the races she saw White Rabbit, Crab, Pigeon, March Hare, and Mad Hatter. She already knew Slug and Drone, and now she saw a turkey, a cuckoo, and a menacing-looking, skinny, stick-like insect with two pairs of arms and hands.

Ostrich and Parrot were there to help Red Dean organize the races. Dragon Lady summoned all the contestants. 'Don't fight the system, folks,' she said. 'The system is good.' And she arranged various faculty members for the first race. She seemed to have no course marked out, but she did have a list of contestants and was summoning whoever was nearby.

'Where's the starting point?' asked Turkey Lurkey. He had a scrawny neck with bags of loose skin on either side. Alix recognized him as the faculty member with the heavy briefcase and transparency problem. As she watched, he tilted his head until it was horizontal, then he seemed to adjust his focus, weaving his head up and down to see clearly.

'Turkey's got his contacts in sideways again,' commented Slug to Alix. 'He's never learned to tell which side of his contact lenses is for reading, which side is for viewing, so he often puts them in sideways. Sometimes I don't think he even knows they're sideways.'

'Turkey Lurkey has a winning attitude but no brains,' said Drone. 'He's won promotion, but I'll never understand how.' Drone jumped over a mud hole.

'Are you sure mud is safe to wallow in these days?' asked Pigeon. She had a round breast and short legs, and

Alix also recognized her from the assembly. Pigeon looked as though she dreaded mud of any kind as she carefully stepped over a mud puddle. Alix saw that Henny Penny was with Pigeon, trying even harder to avoid the mud, carrying a ladder to span the puddles by creating a personal bridge. The upcoming race seemed to be mostly for the birds, so Dragon Lady called for Henny Penny, Pigeon, Turkey Lurkey, and Chanticlaret. Alix had not yet met Chanticlaret and wondered what she would look like.

Red Dean stood on a podium and announced: 'Now hear this! For the sake of an orderly race, I am requesting that you refrain from unnecessary bleating, braying, squeaking, screeching, mooing, neighing, grunting, growling, barking, chirping, hooting, honking, clucking, hissing, and quacking.'

The faculty members were just as confused as Alix about the racecourse. Many were milling about, many were stretching, and most were making the characteristic noises forbidden by Red Dean. Being birds, they chirped, squawked, twittered, and peeped. Dragon Lady marked out the course in a sort of circle. 'The exact shape doesn't matter,' she said when Pigeon asked whether the course was a circle or an oval. Meanwhile Red Dean designated several runners and sent them to the course, which was marked with orange traffic cones and green flags with numbers.

'What about all this mud?' asked Henny Penny. 'What are they trying to do, drown us?' Clutching her ladder firmly, she lined up near Pigeon. Not only was the ladder a bridge for puddles, it was also a shield against being bumped and, if necessary, a means of climbing out of deep puddles or streams. She never raced without it.

The last contestant to arrive, a plump broody hen named Chanticlaret, kept asking everyone she met, 'Don't you think I have a musical voice? Everyone always says I have a musical voice.' So that everyone might appreciate her musical tones, she lightly tapped three notes on her small set of chimes she carried. Sure enough, the chimes matched her voice tones. She wore a pastel shirtwaist dress that emphasized her bosom nicely, being snug and high waisted.

Duck and Goose were deep in conversation and paid no attention to the race. Others paid more attention to themselves than to Dragon Lady's instructions. 'Cuckoo and I are struggling with our roles,' said a stick-shaped insect with skinny arms and legs and an angular head.

'Who's that?' asked Alix. She had found Slug and Drone standing on a rock away from the mud, apparently intending to avoid the mud races if they could.

'Preying Praying Mantis,' said Slug. 'Keep your distance from it.' Slug allowed his body to flow back to the size of a slug, the better to hide.

'Why?' asked Alix. 'It looks harmless. It's hard to believe those little arms could harm anyone.'

Indeed, it did look harmless as it tilted its head from one side to another and waved its hands in the air in front of its face. 'I don't know where the course is!' it said. 'I don't know how to race! I don't know where the race is!' It seemed to be very distressed indeed.

'No one does,' said Dragon Lady. 'Just stand there.' She assigned positions to various animals by placing them somewhere on the course. Slug, Crab, Cuckoo, Pigeon, and others were given spots, but Slug shrunk even smaller and slid off into a discarded track shoe, where he hid. Alix, being taller than many contestants, could see that the course *was* confused, having nothing to indicate starting line, direction, finish line, or the course itself. She wondered how anyone could hope to follow the course.

Slug turned to Turkey Lurkey, who was jogging in place beside him, and said, 'Haven't you run this race before? I've nothing personal against fitness, but you're turning into a jock.' As Turkey Lurkey then ran in tight circles, Slug tried to avoid being squashed by his feet. Alix saw that Turkey's head was tilted over even more, so his contacts must be upside down, or nearly so.

Many other animals had raced before, in previous years, so they began running where they liked. Pigeon said, 'The thing is, I've done this before, and I'm very good at it, whether I run or fly, even though I'm quite small.' As though to prove it, she ran in tight figure eights. And, as if to emphasize her size, she wore a schoolgirl jumper and hair ribbons. She looked like a star fifth-grade pupil from several decades ago.

Henny Penny threw up her wings and said, 'I can't fly! I'll be stomped into the mud! I can't use the ladder for every puddle in the race, because then I'd really be over-run! Run over!'

Red Dean shouted, 'In the interest of safety, pay attention. If you have to brake hard for an emergency, the racer behind you may not be able to stop as fast. So leave plenty of space between you and the racer following you.' Alix thought the danger was more likely to come from head-on crashes, the way the contestants were moving.

Turkey Lurkey challenged Goose and Duck. 'Watch out, Goose, this is it. We're going to give you a chance to show what you can do on a *really* fast track.' Being both a contestant and a minor official in the races, Turkey Lurkey enjoyed officiating because he was so officious, but his competitive spirits usually prevailed. He recognized this, as he mentioned to Duck, 'I have the weirdest feeling that someone was fiddling with my genes last night.'

Goose said, 'Did you hear that? Turkey is already finding excuses. Then again, his contacts are upside down, so he can't see the mud. To him, it's all a brown blur.'

Duck quacked softly to Goose, 'Watch out! Here comes Turkey. He plays to win.' Duck and Goose ambled away from Turkey Lurkey. They got into the group of chickens and other smaller birds. Soon they regretted it a bit, for Pigeon and Cuckoo were among the runners. Alix thought the racecourse was even more confusing now—it was impossible to tell who was a contestant, who was trying to avoid competing, and where the race began.

'Watch me!' said Cuckoo. 'I have such cool feathers!'

'Why can't you be real?' Pigeon liked being the center of attention herself, Alix had noticed. Pigeon wore sub-dued colors, but she constantly told everyone how smart she was. Alix saw that Cuckoo had such *hot* feathers—bright red, electric blue, coal black, glowing green, sulfurous gold. There was nothing subdued or sub-hued about Cuckoo.

Pigeon decided to cool Cuckoo down. 'Have you nested yet?' She asked, knowing the answer was no, but that Cuckoo was nest- and mate-hunting.

Cuckoo wandered off towards what she thought was the center of the course, looking for Mr. Good-nest.

Pigeon followed. 'The thing is, I've always made superior nests.' But she was not good at running in mud, for she slipped and fell in a huge mudhole and disappeared from sight.

'Look at me!' shouted Cuckoo. 'I'm running! Wow! Like, you know, really running!'

'Why doesn't she fly?' asked Alix, watching as Cuckoo splattered more and more mud on her once-bright feathers.

'She's convinced that running is more interesting for everyone to watch,' said Goose. 'Besides, she always out-runs Pigeon and Duck. They have such short legs.'

'So she wants to be interesting?' Alix asked. 'To whom?'

'To potential lovers,' answered Drone. 'She wants to nest, but you know what cuckoos are. They don't build nests. They appropriate others' nests.'

'Has she found a lover yet?' asked Alix. She thought that such a brightly colored bird must attract a lot of suitors.

'No one wants her in their nest. She thinks she has to become more interesting and then she'll be welcome. That's why she colors her feathers so brightly and changes the colors often. She dyes her feathers different colors so she can fascinate and capture a mate.'

Cuckoo's next comment sounded like a response. 'I'm very fussy when it comes to a mate.'

Drone said, 'Yes, she likes two kinds of males, domestic and foreign.' Once again he was glad he wasn't an eligible bird as he carefully folded his wings out of her sight. No point in drawing attention to wings with Cuckoo around.

'Look at me!' screamed Cuckoo. 'I'm doing the hokey pokey!'

Pigeon said, 'Would you be interested in a battle of wits, instead of a race?' Still drenched with mud, Pigeon was shivering and stinky, but she didn't dare withdraw, not if she hoped to rise in Red Dean's estimation and keep her job.

Meanwhile, somehow, when no one was paying attention, the race began. All the other birds and animals were running higgledy-piggledy because no one had told them where to run or when to stop. The exact dimensions of the course, or even inexact dimensions, still were a mystery to everyone. The whole field being a sea of mud, the flags and cones were no help in indicating the course. Besides, the numbers on the flags were too muddy to read. Red Dean and Dragon Lady were shouting directions from more or less the middle of the flock of runners. Instead of telling the runners where the course was, they pointed in various directions and sent contestants around the cones, some in one direction, some in another. The squawking and screeching, crying and moaning added to the chaos. No one knew where to go or who was in charge. Wet and muddy feathers smelled bad, worse, and worst.

Turkey Lurkey and Preying Praying Mantis struggled for what each thought was the lead. They weren't sure because the layout of the race was primarily in the imagination of Red Dean. Preying Praying Mantis's hands were clutched in a predator grip, then they opened, ready to strike and grab, which they did, at Turkey, causing him to swerve, and keeping him from passing.

'It looks as though Praying Mantis will kill and eat Turkey,' said Alix. Just then she saw Mantis lunge forward, once again grabbing at Turkey Lurkey.

'I don't think she'll eat him,' said Slug. 'She eats only lemons.' Slug was still hiding in a track shoe.

'She?' said Alix. 'It's a she? Does she win races?'

'She thinks so,' said Slug. 'She's always saying she wins because she's pure, because she believes in fairness and equality, in autonomy, in love, in the best one winning. And in her mind, she's the purest, the best.' He peeped out of his shoe to see where the racers were.

'She sounds like Red Dean,' said Alix, keeping an eye on the racers. It was hard to know who was ahead because it was impossible to be sure where the track was.

'Oh, she's a dean-in-waiting,' said Drone. His wings fluttered very fast when he was excited, and something about Preying Praying Mantis agitated him, even though technically he and Mantis were on the same team, both being flying insects.

Slug added, 'Like Red Dean, she's for autonomy, so long as everyone does what she wants. Like Red Dean, she believes in political correctness, that everyone must guard against saying the wrong thing.' Slug had learned it was important to avoid being mistaken for a loose tongue.

'And must belong to exactly the right political party,' said Drone.

'The right?' asked Alix. 'The right wing?' Alix looked at Drone's wings and hoped he understood she wasn't referring to real wings.

'Her right. Technically labeled the left-of-center,' said Drone. He folded his wings and stood up much taller so he hardly resembled a bee at all.

'And vote for the candidates she approves of,' said Slug, also standing taller, now out of the shoe and hydrant-sized again.

As Alix watched Praying Mantis leap onto Turkey's back and grab his head, she asked Drone, 'Is she successful in the races?' Mantis was reaching for Turkey's eyes.

'She's equally successful in political races and in Red Dean's races,' said Slug. 'It's not speed that matters. It's pleasing Red Dean. Red Dean picks the winners.'

Praying Mantis was leaning over Turkey's head and saying in his ear, 'Don't get me wrong, Turkey. I like you, but you're not a special person. I'm a special person.' She covered his eyes and forced his head to turn toward the side. Since Turkey's head was already somewhat sideways in order to see, it was now truly crooked. Perhaps his eyes were towards the rear. Alix thought this handicap might not hurt Turkey as much as it seemed, since no one knew where the racecourse was anyhow. Turkey might as well look backwards as forwards.

By now, Alix saw that Red Dean had declared the first race over. Bugs and birds were scattered all over the racecourse. As Red Dean selected winners, Dragon Lady handed out the prizes. Pigeon received a grant. Preying Praying Mantis got promotion and tenure. Cuckoo was given a raise since Red Dean recognized her posturing as childish, not a threat to order. Dragon Lady, for her expertise in Marxist democracy, got a black belt in kung fu.

Some of the others looked stunned. Henny Penny was running faster than during the race, and she looked more distressed than ever. 'They're going to race us to death! I know it!'

Turkey, because his windpipe had been squeezed shut by Praying Mantis, was speechless. Having raced before,

Slug and Drone nodded, knowing the usual outcomes. Pigeon and Cuckoo were quite muddy and befouled. Everyone looked and smelled like a mud-person.

'Why didn't I win something?' asked Crab. Alix saw him stuck in the muddy field and thought he must be the most optimistic crab that ever lived if he thought he had a chance to win.

'Roland Barthes was struck and killed by a laundry truck as he left the French Institute,' said Dragon Lady. 'Consider yourself lucky.'

'What a system!' said Crab. 'What kind of consolation is that?'

'Don't fight the system, Crab. The system is good,' said Dragon Lady. 'After all, we let you race with the bugs. As Red Dean said, "What's a crab anyway, but a bigger bug?" '

Slug hid behind Drone as Dragon Lady looked towards them.

'Red Dean should be called Dead Duck Dean,' said Drone. 'Her political influence is waning.' Drone tried to get behind Slug, but Slug had shrunk again.

'We used to have a revolving deaconry,' said Slug, 'but when her turn came she wouldn't revolve out.' Slug revolved on his tail, showing how easy revolving was.

Preying Praying Mantis wobbled past, talking to Caterpillar. 'I tried to have fun, as you told me to.' She seemed too heavy for her stick legs, even though she was thin as a small twig.

'At least you made it from larva to pupa to adult,' said Caterpillar. 'I stopped at pupa, or is it larva? I'll have to think it over.' He paused and puffed his pipe and seemed to think some more.

'Just because I'm not laughing doesn't mean I don't get it,' said Praying Mantis. 'Laughing takes a lot of energy.' She swayed and almost fell over as she spoke.

'Who's joking?' asked Caterpillar. 'We're both struggling with our roles.'

Along came Cuckoo. 'I had a role. I tried being myself, but it wasn't getting me anywhere.' She fluffed her feathers. 'I'm bored.' She had mud splotches all over her feathers. Alix wanted to suggest that Cuckoo go shower off the mud and stench.

'This won't bore you,' said Red Dean. 'Begin the next race, everyone!'

Alix slipped around the course, trying to dodge runners, and mudholes, and mudhens. This time the course was marked with steeplechase gates, barrels, and even a sand trap! Red Dean had ordered three truckloads of sand for one section of the course. Alix thought the whole course could use some sand. She ducked as Mantis tottered by, munching a dark object. 'What's that?' Alix asked. 'I thought she only ate lemons.' Alix saw that the object was furry and quite dark.

'Lemons, and an occasional head,' said Drone. 'Why do you think she's called *preying*?'

Alix was confused. 'I thought she was the praying mantis.'

'She's both,' said Drone. 'She preys with the first set of hands, and prays with the next pair.' He put the tips of his wings together like praying hands. 'That's why she developed a second set of claws. Most mantises have only one pair. She's got two!'

'What prayers?' Alix kept a wary eye out for Mantis. She didn't want to become prey bait or prayer bait. Just then Preying Praying Mantis finished her last bite and tilted her head to get a bead on Alix. Alix ducked behind Goose, who was taller than Drone and Slug.

'She prays for peace,' said Goose, 'for understanding. For cooperation.' His wing-hands looked graceful in prayer position, and he often held them that way, especially when he wore his Roman collar. Fewer people hollered at him then.

'Does she believe in those things?' asked Alix as she avoided Mantis's clutch.

'She thinks she does, and you'd better believe in those same things,' said Drone, sliding to his left to avoid Preying Mantis. 'Or—'

'No head,' said Alix, unconsciously reaching for her head to make sure it was okay.

'No head. Gone. She'll get it,' agreed Drone, Slug, and Goose. Goose stood on tiptoe, spread his wings, and everyone hid behind them. 'Her control method is primitive but effective.'

Praying Mantis overheard them. 'Shut up! I'm always considerate.'

'Yeah, right,' said Goose. 'Lucky you can't hear my interior monologue.'

'When I get the chance I'm going to sock you,' said Preying Praying Mantis.

Alix watched with relief as Mantis moved on. 'What does she teach?' Alix hoped she would never have to take a class with Praying Mantis. She began thinking of several of her high school teachers, and how nice they seemed now. She was scared of several of these professors, certainly of Preying Praying Mantis.

'She teaches weaving,' said Slug. 'She's wonderful at it herself.' He swayed from side to side as he thought of a loom.

'She's better than any spider,' added Goose. He normally avoided spiders, and he closed his eyes tightly at the thought of finding one on a loom.

Putting her hands in her pockets at the thought of spiders nearby, Alix asked, 'Does she like spiders?'

'No, they won't do the designs she wants,' answered Goose, 'so she eats their heads.' He shivered violently.

Slug shuddered. 'No one ever told her that the spider heads aren't lemons, because she'd eat their heads, too.'

'Was she promoted because of her weaving?'

'Well,' said Drone, 'she and Red Dean have the same pattern, so she was promoted.'

'Have?' asked Alix. 'What do you mean, "have the same pattern"?'

'The patterns are internalized,' explained Drone, 'the exact, precise way to do things, to speak, to act, to dress, to pray. Anyone who doesn't conform to the patterns is removed.'

'Removed from what?' Alix was trying to see how this conformed to all the talk of autonomy and fairness. And community! And love! She looked again at Preying Praying Mantis, who seemed so frail. Why did Red Dean reward her? What was the secret to her success? She seemed incompetent and unsure of herself. The selection of winners was as confusing as the races were.

Slug answered, 'Their computers are removed.' He would have shrugged if he'd had shoulders, or arms. As it was, his whole body shrugged in an odd accordion movement.

'Then they are removed from the staff,' said Goose. 'Look, over there in the shade is a Removed. That person is writing a satire about us.'

'Oh,' said Alix, 'you said that person. Isn't that phrase banned?'

'We have to say *that person* in this case,' said Goose. 'Red Dean removed that person's name from the roster and forbid us to say it.'

Chanticlaret and Henny Penny came by, looking for the next race since they were both unsure of the outcome of the previous race, and both thought they had better race again. But it had already begun, of course, and the contestants were running, jumping, hopping, leaping, and panting. Some were exhausted, lying on the ground and heaving. Pigeon was hopping about on one leg. Alix thought that everyone might be better off if Red Dean would just tell them where the race began, and whether to run or jump, and which direction to run, and when to stop. Something about the frantic racing about reminded

Alix of Keystone Kops movies, with so much frenzied activity, so much pointless running about. But in this confused race, with everyone so anxious, she dared not laugh. 'Why is everyone so distressed?' she asked Drone.

'Careers are at stake. Promotions. Tenure. Salaries. Raises. Grants. Premium offices. New computers that actually work. Their whole lives.' Drone looked peaked as he listed the stakes. Alix saw that all, even the reluctant faculty, had to participate in the races if they hoped to have jobs. It meant that tiny Slug and Drone had to race Turkey and Preying Praying Mantis. She wondered whether she would meet any faculty who avoided the contests altogether. Was anyone that brave? Or was it foolhardy?

On the course, some animals were tripping each other. Some were leapfrogging—the frogs and toads had a big advantage there. A frog said to a lizard, 'You're always wearing your jumpsuit, but you never jump. Look at our success,' and he jumped over several beavers. 'You should watch this. You might learn something.'

A toad landed on the frog and pinned him down. 'For years I was afraid of overconfidence, but when I finally gave in to it, it wasn't bad at all.'

The frog said, 'When people ask what you're like, I say you're a saint. That usually shuts them up.' He shook the toad off and pulled himself out of the mud.

Cuckoo was huffing along, talking as usual to her audience, who ignored her. 'Like, you know, I mean, sometimes I wonder about how I'm doing, you know!' Her audience consisted of Pigeon and Henny Penny, who were also her competitors, if this was truly the race. Dragon Lady kept gathering more and more contestants. Probably the race had not yet officially begun.

Pigeon, her feathers hardly visible beneath the mud, was saying to Henny Penny, 'I told him I decided to leave him, but he doesn't seem able to take it in. He's committed to the ideal of the perfect family.'

Henny Penny, hearing that comment, replied, 'Everyone in our family has a commitment to something. I hope Red Dean doesn't break up our families. She's been trying. They don't want us to be happy.'

The fowl race was going more smoothly than the frog jumping. For one thing, Chanticlaret preferred to speak rather than compete, and so did Cuckoo and Pigeon. The trouble was, each one of them wanted an audience and none of them wanted to *be* an audience. But at least they weren't fighting or landing on each other.

Even though both wore strapless organdy dresses with several puffy petticoats, Mad Hatter and March Hare easily outpaced other animals, both in running and in jumping. Mad Hatter, a stocky woman, wore a yellow dress and hat, while March Hare, taller and more nimble, wore a green dress and hat. Pausing to shake water out of her yellow high heels, Mad Hatter asked, 'Ever kind of wonder what we should do next with our might?' Both stopped to watch the others behind them. 'We've always been the fastest, but do we get the mostest? Nooooo!'

Smoothing out her skirts, March Hare asked, 'When do we get to choose our prizes?'

'When did we ever get to choose?' asked Mad Hatter. 'What else would Red Dean do with her time? She makes all the choices.' She adjusted her hat so it wouldn't fall into the muddy course. It was very yellow, very glossy, covered with feathers, and very low over her forehead. It looked like a beret with feathers.

At that moment Alix saw Dodo and Dragon Lady wade into the middle of the racecourse. The contestants who were still standing, or running, or jumping began to try even harder. Alix said to Goose, 'Why are they trying so hard if the results don't matter? You said that Red Dean picks winners by whim instead of by speed.'

'Yes, but this determines how she sees them,' said Goose. 'Their careers and lives are at stake.' Goose no longer believed the official line, that the institution was a meritocracy.

'Don't they have lives outside the institution?'

'Outside the institution? Are you crazy? Red Dean wouldn't allow it.' Goose looked shocked. 'Everyone is on twenty-four-hour call via E-mail.' To emphasize this point he lifted his briefcase containing his laptop.

'On call to her?'

'On call to all students, students who might want to talk to their professors or their advisors. Everyone must have their computer on at all times so that all messages get through immediately! The machines are programmed to ensure that messages from the campus cannot be deleted in groups. That's one of Red Dean's commands.' Goose checked his laptop for messages.

At that moment Ostrich called out, 'The race is over!' and everyone who hadn't already quit stopped now. Then he said, 'I move that the meeting be adjourned.'

'Ostrich seems to have very little to do,' commented Alix, watching him wander around. 'Does he think this is a meeting or a race?'

'He's out of the loop, he says,' said Drone, making loops with his hands.

Slug moved through the crowd toward them. 'Time for Red Dean to distribute wins. Always a surprise.' He found a concrete culvert and sat on it so he could see.

Alix said, 'I thought you all told me that she had predetermined the winners. What's the surprise?'

'They don't know what the criteria are,' said Duck. 'Last year she told the jumpers that vertical distance, not height, was the object of pole vaulting.'

'By the time they realized that vertical distance and height are the same thing, she had already selected her winners,' said Slug, now the size of a corner mail box.

'That's why Turkey Lurkey won the jumping contest over Frog and Toad,' said Goose. 'Even though they both jumped higher and farther.'

Red Dean announced, 'These paradigm shifts occurred while you were out on the course,' as she gave grants to Janus JekyllHyde, White Rabbit, and Turkey Lurkey. She named Drone a Distinguished Fellow, Slug an Honorary Fellow, Goose a Distinguished Fowl, Duck an Honorary Fowl, and Cuckoo a Regular Fowl.

'Honorary Fowl! I'm a real fowl,' cried Duck. 'Every year she gives me some honorary title instead of a grant. I've won a dozen national grants, but never a grant from inside the institution. Turkey and Janus get those.'

'How can anyone think Cuckoo is regular?' Alix asked. 'And where was Janus JekyllHyde during the race? I never saw him. Did he really run at all?' She looked around at the contestants and realized it was hard to actually see anyone beneath the mud.

'She's picked out her favorites again,' said Slug. 'Actually, this isn't as bad as the punishments she dishes out to those she has a grudge against. Wait till you see that.' At the thought of the punishments he'd seen, he contracted his body again.

Henny Penny got a prize, a desk. 'All my life I've wanted a big desk. Now that I've got it, what do I want? A big pen.' She looked at the desk, then noticed it was a rolltop. 'I'll get caught in the top and smother! I'll suffocate in there! They're trying to stifle me!'

Red Dean awarded cupboards to March Hare, saying, 'Cupboards offer storage space.'

'Oh, good,' said March Hare, 'they'll do fine for me instead of a lab.' March Hare continued to hope, in spite of everything, that productive faculty might be rewarded fairly.

Dragon Lady said, 'She only gave me chattels and movables!'

Red Dean heard that. 'The words "chattels" and "movables" may sound funny to you, but I assure you they refer to some pretty serious things.' Alix saw Dragon Lady tremble.

Dragon Lady muttered, 'Nothing works here, not even total obedience. I thought that if I obeyed all the time, in all things, Red Dean would reward me.' Her wings drooped as her spirits dropped. She had tried for so long to please Red Dean in all matters, only to be scorned.

Red Dean was unsympathetic. 'If only the artist were up to the atelier.'

'What on earth does that mean?' asked Dragon Lady. Alix thought that Red Dean was just trying to demoralize and confuse Dragon Lady, but she didn't want to say so.

Red Dean told Dragon Lady, 'You have a winning attitude but apparently no guts. Now get aboard. Join the team—Turkey Lurkey has escaped into optimism. You can too.'

Dragon Lady said softly, 'I awoke with deep foreboding this morning. And now I'm going to be removed, I know it.' She seemed dejected, rejected after all her help during the races.

Red Dean's last award was a cap and gown for White Rabbit. 'It's wrinkle-free, wash-and-wear, stain-resistant, and bulletproof,' she said as she handed it to him.

Ostrich said to the others, 'If you're in favor of a stiff upper lip, raise your hand.' Alix now understood Ostrich —his position was safe, since he was the figurehead at the top. Red Dean kept him out of the loop, but he did not have to do anything to please her. No wonder he wore a birthday crown from Burger King. A perfect symbol of his invulnerability.

'How many lips do you see out there?' Mad Hatter asked. 'Hares have lips, mostly harelips, so those aren't stiff. The others, forget it.'

'I see lots of stiff upper beaks, though,' said March Hare, looking at Pigeon, Cuckoo, Turkey, and Henny

Penny. Chanticlaret's beak was open wide, for she sang as she accompanied herself with chimes.

'Well, the faculty races are over again for the summer,' said Drone. 'Why do I always hope for something?' Drone still hoped for a real race one year, with clearly marked tracks, an established finish line, and prizes distributed for merit. 'Mad Hatter tried to tell me not to expect anything, but I didn't listen to her. After Mad Hatter figured out what was going on, Red Dean said she was mad. Red Dean hasn't been able to control Mad Hatter, or March Hare, but she's tried to control our opinion of them by describing them as mad and by overlooking them at awards time. They'll never get grants if Red Dean can help it, no matter how many papers they read at professional meetings, no matter how much they publish in national journals.'

'What else is there left for us?' asked Slug. 'We'll never win awards with Red Dean around. How long will she have the deaconry?'

Mad Hatter said, 'You've been here long enough to know that deans stay forever. They are above evaluations, above reviews, above races, above time itself.'

'No wonder Red Dean calls you mad,' said Alix, who liked Mad Hatter and March Hare, but she could see why Red Dean wouldn't. They saw too much.

Alix now thought of her cat, Dinah, named after Alice's cat. She held her breath and thought of Dinah and Lily and Eleanor. She thought of Tim, and of her father. She wished she had left with Eleanor.

Where was Eleanor anyway? Alix could not remember seeing Eleanor leave, but she was gone. If this was a dream, why couldn't she see whom she wanted? Why couldn't she even see a vision of them? She'd never seen anything as confusing as these mud races, where no one knew where the course was, or which direction to run, or where the starting point was, or where the finish was, and to make it all worse, everyone's career depended on the race. If Red Dean had her way, their whole *lives* would hang on the outcome.

With the annual faculty mud races over, Ostrich summoned everyone inside to view his transparencies. He removed them from his briefcase—all seven of them and carefully put them—all seven at once—on the projector.

The writing overlapped, of course, and nothing was readable.

Turkey Lurkey huffed. 'He's no expert like I am. That's why I put my transparencies on the projector one at a time.'

Alix asked Slug, 'What is he an expert on again?'

'You name it—assemblies, relationships, harassment, races, fantasies, but mostly self-promotion. And now, it seems, overhead projectors.'

'Wasn't he the person in the assembly who had to put his transparency on diagonally?' asked Alix. 'Everyone laughed.'

'Yes, but it was done *expertly*. Just ask him.'

Turkey Lurkey then turned to Ostrich. 'I noticed that each of your last three press releases began with the phrase, "It strains credulity . . ." '

Alix asked Drone, 'Is that why Turkey is so close to Red Dean, because he is such an expert?'

Goose answered instead. 'He follows her patterns; he's her favorite follower. He praises everything she does; she rewards him with salary. He was promoted and granted, granted and promoted; now he's got the top rank and the top salary. All she can give him is more and more praise and influence, and more grants.' Alix thought of Alice having to provide the prizes after the caucus races, and she was relieved she wouldn't have to. No one in this group would be satisfied with thimbles and candies from her pockets. They were too mature, or perhaps too immature.

Mad Hatter suddenly sang out, 'Gather round, everyone, for my song and she climbed onto the tea cart she had driven to the races and began singing:

There was a Young Scholar, or Singing in Tongues

There was a young scholar, heigh-ho,
There was a young scholar from Bremen,
Wrote a book on the end of her toe.
Ta-tum, ta-tum, ta-tum!
There was a young scholar from Bremen
Wrote on the left cheek of her bum
A paean to administrators,
A hymn to the best of the best,
To those bold administrators
Who live in the land of the blest,
Who always have jam with their coffee,
Who always eat toast with their tea,
Who always seek our best interests,
Who always get paid three
Times whatever a scholar
Gets paid for her didilly-dum:
So wrote the young scholar from Bremen
On the lovely left cheek of her bum.

Alix saw in the back of the course many animals and birds who had not won. Most of them seemed in need of a prize, some sort of consolation. Their feathers were more matted than ever. Others had muddy fur. A beaver was saying, 'I remember *nothing* that I learned in high school.' Alix decided he was incoherent, though it was hard to tell, because she had heard so many incoherent things.

As she looked around, everyone seemed stunned. She wanted to tell them about the rules they should follow to please Red Dean. She wondered why no one told them about the correct ways and means. She wondered why they stayed here at all.

Along came White Rabbit, checking his watch again. He was saying to himself, 'I've got to get to Caedmon Hall as soon as possible. What time is it now?'

'You speak English!' cried Alix. She felt she knew him already.

'Of course I speak English. Doesn't everyone?' He glanced at his watch and shook it.

Alix was puzzled. 'The last time I saw you, you were saying, "*Quelle heure est'il?*"—I assumed you were French.' She thought of how much he resembled the drawings of the white rabbit she had often looked at in *Alice in Wonderland*.

'French!?!' said White Rabbit. 'The French are imbeciles! How could you think I am French? Do you take me for an imbecile?'

'I don't know you,' said Alix as calmly as she could. She didn't want to excite him any more than he already was.

'Then why do you think I am an imbecile?' White Rabbit was already quite excited.

'I don't think you're an imbecile—'

'Then why do you think I'm French?' the rabbit demanded. 'The French are imbeciles.'

Alix gave up. The conversation was too stressful. Fortunately, White Rabbit looked at his watch again. 'I'm late! I'm late for Caedmon.'

Chapter Four

Bats in the Belfry
and Loose Marbles

"Curiouser and curiouser,' said Alix, consciously quoting Alice. 'How queer everything is today.' She saw a feathered figure approaching. It was familiar but she wasn't sure who it was. The feathers were oddly askew, rumpled, twisted, and broken. Also, they were several unnatural colors—chiefly hot pink, puce, chartreuse. In some spots they were missing altogether, a result of intense dyeing, Alix thought. Then Alix recognized the odd twitches and jerky movements. It was Cuckoo.

'Alix, I've been sent to give you a tour of the classrooms. We'll start here with Windy Hole.'

'Do you mean Windy Hall?' asked Alix. She zipped her jacket and shouldered her backpack.

'No, Windy Hole. You'll see.' Cuckoo gave a little hop as she started off for the nearest building.

Indeed, Alix did see, as soon as they got inside. The stairs to the lower level were right inside the entrance, and Cuckoo led Alix down, down, into dark narrow corridors. Soon Alix could barely see Cuckoo's brightest feathers. She hoped Cuckoo knew the way. It was hard to tell with Cuckoo when she was disoriented and when she was normal. Alix saw other corridors, some even smaller and darker than the one they were in. She saw many doors, most of them with names or labels or numbers to identify them, but it was too dark to read them. Some of the labels she could see made no sense, and the numbers were not in sequence.

In some echoing chambers off a corridor, people were speaking. The sounds were muffled, perhaps because of the curves. As Cuckoo led her down a branch of the corridor she saw a grotto with life-sized evergreen shrubs shaped like various birds—penguins, cranes, ravens, crows, and ducks. 'Models of retired faculty,' Cuckoo assured her, 'wonderful memorials; someday all this will be part of your personal mythology.'

Alix thought she also saw some mummies. 'Is this some sort of catacomb?' Feeling apprehensive, she did not want to follow Cuckoo further into the curving corridors, but she knew she could not find her way out. She was unsure of Cuckoo's guiding abilities. Alix felt hotter as she walked farther into the cave-like lower level. She removed her windbreaker, tied it around her waist, and tucked her hat into the jacket. Her ID bracelet from Tim broke off and fell just as Cuckoo turned another corner, but Alix didn't notice as she raced after Cuckoo.

Alix caught up with Cuckoo and they came to a large, dark classroom. 'Art mystery,' said Cuckoo, 'a popular class.' Alix saw many students sitting in the gloom looking at a large screen in the front of the room.

The art mystery professor spoke from the darkest corner of the room: 'Some damned fine stuff here. But it lacks a sense of adventure. I want you to start . . .' But Cuckoo moved on before Alix could hear the rest of the sentence. As she moved quickly to catch up with Cuckoo, she did not notice her jacket and hat falling off.

Alix never saw the art mystery professor, but she did see the next professor, a short, voluptuous woman wearing a long, tight-fitting dress, black with white ruffles in the front, and an enormous black hat with a white ostrich feather, and very high heels. 'She's Mae East, the sociolocopathology professor,' whispered Cuckoo. Alix saw dozens and dozens of students in the room taking up all the available seats, perching on the podium, on the radiator, leaning against the back wall, standing in the doorway. Some sat on others' laps. On the blackboard Mae East wrote the title of her lecture: The Haves and the Have-Nots.

Alix felt for her jacket. 'My windbreaker!' she cried. 'My hat!'

'Your what?' asked Cuckoo absently. She was not paying attention to Alix. Why should she? She had feathers to keep her warm, most of her feathers anyway. Alix tried to find her jacket and hat, then noticed Cuckoo leaving, turning down yet another corridor. In the dark Alix felt around with her hands and feet. She had lost her sense of direction in the many corridors they had been through. She had no idea which way she had come, or which way to get out. She saw a dim glow and moved in that direction. It turned out to be another grotto.

'Someday I'd like to make this my private study,' said Cuckoo, 'but right now it's Mae's.' Alix jumped, startled to find Cuckoo was with her.

'Where are we?' asked Alix. 'Is this the way out?'

Cuckoo turned into another corridor, then into a smaller room. Alix saw a group of professors, or people she assumed were professors by their long black frock coats and knowing manner. Alix thought they were going into a lounge because two of them were smoking big cigars, but they all went into a classroom and Cuckoo followed them and motioned for Alix to follow her. There was plenty of room for Cuckoo and Alix in the classroom, for it contained only three students. Alix saw all five professors standing in a row in the front.

'We'll watch this class,' said Cuckoo. 'I knew they'd have room for us.' Again she gave a little hop, then led Alix to a desk in the rear of the room.

'How did you know?' asked Alix. She sat in one of the many empty chairs.

'It's a Frong class. All Frong classes have room because they don't have many students.' The professors lined up in front of the blackboard. The three students, feeling outnumbered, as they were, looked at the five professors. The first professor began writing a list of Frong verbs and their endings on the board, the second wrote Frong adjectives with their articles, the third wrote Frong pronouns, the fourth listed Frong nouns with the proper articles, and the fifth explained everything.

'Who are they?' asked Alix. She looked at each of the professors.

'The Frong brothers—Groucho, Chico, Gummo, Harpo, and Zeppo.'

'The Frong brothers? Is that their name?'

'Convenient, isn't it?' said Cuckoo. 'They're named Frong and they teach Frong. Red Dean says they've got their act together.'

'Why so many?' asked Alix. 'Is Frong that hard?' She thought of the incredible number of students in the sociolocopathology class, and of the name of the lecture on the board. She had certainly seen the Have-Nots and the Haves.

'They need five,' said Cuckoo. 'Harpo doesn't talk, as you may remember. Everyone ignores and forgets Gummo.

Zeppo is around only as a romantic lead, Chico is unreliable. That leaves Groucho to do all the explaining.'

This sounded reasonable to Alix, as reasonable as anything else she had heard here. Maybe she was more tired than she realized, she thought. She was lost, dazed and confused, and disoriented. Cuckoo did not seem at all sure where the stairs were. How would they find their way out in the dark? Were these classes typical? Were any classes of normal size?

'They're very thorough,' said Cuckoo, gesturing toward the Frong brothers. 'And they teach fast!'

'They should be!' exclaimed Alix. 'Five professors in one class!'

All five brothers suddenly turned toward her. 'We'd like to know what, in your opinion, makes you think you're so hot.' This time, all five spoke.

Alix was hot, so she took off her sweatshirt, wrapped it around her waist, and knotted it. Tightly, she hoped. All she had left was her SPAM T-shirt.

'Why don't you all speak Frong?' she asked the Frong professors.

'We teach Frong, we don't speak it,' they said together.

Alix found Cuckoo by the door of the classroom. 'Can you get me out? I'm feeling weird, sort of dizzy.'

'Of course. The rules are clearly established. No one can be a guide unless she knows every street, alley, corner, and neighborhood.' Cuckoo gave two little hops this time.

'But do you know the buildings?' Alix looked around but couldn't see anything in the dark, not even an exit sign.

'Let's go this way,' Cuckoo said, and vanished in the gloom. Alix tried to see which direction Cuckoo had gone but the corridors were darker than ever. Then she saw a small glowing disc close to the floor and moving. She felt towards it and heard a 'Meow!'

'Good,' said Alix, 'a real cat. I'll follow it instead.' It led her to an escape clause and she climbed out of the depths of despair. The glowing circle on the cat's collar vanished in the light. Alix could see a window and a door, so she left Windy Hole.

The outside door faced Caedmon Hall. Something was going on there. Or rather going down. Alix saw that the steps were full of creatures rolling down. She heard marbles, Pigeon, Mad Hatter, March Hare, Henny Penny, Crab, Magpie, Drone, and Slug rolling, bouncing, and bounding down the steps onto the ground. Everyone was groaning or squawking or shouting, mostly 'Help!' or 'Ouch!' as Crab, Magpie, and Drone rolled down together in a veritable tangle of wings, claws, and beaks. Marbles glittered in the sunlight, bounced on the steps, on the tangles of screaming birds. 'We're all going to be rolled into one big bird!' shouted Henny Penny.

'The thing is, I've never taken to flying,' said Pigeon as she landed on Goose, who then fell onto Henny Penny, who promptly screamed, 'They're going to flatten us all!' She had abandoned her ladder of protection in the melee, and she was running around dodging marbles and beads and bodies dropping from the windows. Most of the bodies were screaming as they fell, and since most of the inhabitants were birds, they sort of flew down, but Henny Penny was still terrified. 'Squashed to death by birds! Bombarded by beads! Mangled by marbles! They're bombing us!' she cried.

'What happened?' asked Alix running toward all the activity.

'It was Red Dean's loose marbles!' cried Pigeon. 'They began rolling around and soon everyone was falling. Dragon Lady tried to catch herself but caught Cuckoo's beaded curtain door and pulled that loose and then we had even more rolly floors. Then everyone stepped on the loose marbles and loose beads and fell, first on the floor, then down the hall, and finally down the stairs and out of the building.'

'I wasn't even there,' said Cuckoo, hopping up from Windy Hole, fluffing her feathers.

'But your door was, and now it's loose beads.' Pigeon stepped on a marble and fell.

Henny Penny, seeing her fall, began running around in circles. 'They're going to break our legs. They planned this so we would all break our legs! I can't find my ladder!' Just then Henny's ladder popped out of a crack in the outer wall onto Henny's head.

Slug rolled down the last few steps. 'Dragon Lady's bats got loose!' he shouted.

'Bats?' asked Alix, wondering how bats related to marbles.

'The bats in her belfry. They're flying around!' said Slug as he hit the ground.

March Hare came bouncing down the last few steps. 'The bats flew into Cuckoo's candles! Now their wings are on fire!' She landed on the sidewalk with a soft *thud*. Marbles, beads, and bats landed around her in a terrible clatter.

They heard a shout from inside. 'Red Dean came to the rescue!'

'Thank goodness!' said Pigeon. 'She's got lots of hot air inside her. She can blow out the fire.' Pigeon tried to catch Henny Penny, who was still running around and around and screaming. She had hoped to use her ladder to rescue herself and the other inhabitants, but now the building was too hot to approach.

The whole building was soon smoking and flaming. Flames showed through the windows. They could hear fire crackling, glass exploding, and the blaze roaring from room to room, entering each room with a huge *rush* of flame and broken glass and heat. Puffs of smoke came out of every pore, every crack, every wrinkle. 'The old cracks are letting in fresh air!' shouted Goose. 'Now there's a four-way draft!' Huge smoke columns rose from the building, black, bad-smelling, and billowing in several directions.

Firefighters arrived in a yellow blur, rushed up the steps, rolled back down. The firefighters on the other three sides of the building were rolling down the steps also, rolling on the marbles and beads. They shouted, 'Look out below, we're coming down!' Some of them fell on Henny Penny and Pigeon at the foot of the steps. 'I'm going to be smashed by firemen now!' shouted Henny. 'They all have humongous axes! They'll knock my head off!'

'Loose marbles!' the fire chief shouted. 'Who would keep loose marbles?' Just then he stepped on one, his left foot flew into the air, and he landed on Cuckoo. 'Oooooofffda! More marbles rained down on him in a rainbow of crystal, agate, blue, green, red, and yellow.

White Rabbit came running up. 'I'm in charge! I'm in charge! Pull the walls down! We have to get the fire out!' He began running around and around the building, through the smoke, until he too stepped on a marble and fell.

'Not yet,' said the chief, 'Turkey Lurkey is climbing the walls.'

'What else is new?' said Slug. 'We've all been climbing the walls for years.' Slug himself enjoyed climbing walls —it came naturally to him, being a slug.

'We have to reach the second story and the third to fight the fire,' said the chief. 'Our ladders aren't tall enough.' He rubbed his backside where he had fallen on Cuckoo.

'I command the building,' said White Rabbit. 'Here's a step stool. It will extend your reach.' He had a step stool and a large bucket with him.

'How?' asked the chief incredulously, looking at the three-step stool.

'Put it down first, as the bottom ladder, then put your ladders on top.'

'We can't use an extending ladder with a step stool! It will fall off!' said the chief.

'Don't be contrary,' said White Rabbit. 'Tape the ladders together with goose tape.'

'Goose tape? Do you mean duct tape?'

'Goose tape. Duck tape. Loon tape. What's the difference? We're an equal opportunity, affirmative action employer, as long as I'm in charge,' said White Rabbit.

Firefighters on all sides were squirting water into the building through the holes in the walls, the existing cracks, the new cracks made by the fire, even into the windows. The building began to fill with water, groaning at the seams. Alix, who had been standing outside, soon found herself washed into the building along with Duck, Goose, and March Hare, right down into the basement. Alix could hear sobs and gurgles all around. She was swimming with several beavers, an otter, two muskrats, and three alligators. Duck and Goose knew how to float but March Hare was struggling in the current. Alix bobbed into a small office where she was trapped among the computers. She gulped as she took in water, then untied her sweatshirt, kicked off her shoes, dropped her backpack, and swam for the door.

There, Alix saw the residents of the second floor and the third floor pouring down the stairs. Someone bumped her, knocking her back into the computer room in the corner of the basement. Water began swirling around her head. Alix gulped in more water as she tried to swim for the exit door or a crack. The current kept forcing her back. As she went under water once again, she thought of her life so far. I hope I'm not drowning, she thought. That would be a real downer.

But Alix didn't quite drown. She reached the stairs and began climbing out of the basement just as White Rabbit's crew fastened hooks on the building. White Rabbit was still crying, 'Pull the building down! Get the fire out!' He was jumping and hopping, as rabbits do, but not helping with the emergency.

'Doesn't he see the water?' asked Drone. 'Fire is no longer the problem.'

Now, wet residents began flowing out of windows, doors, cracks, and holes as the water overflowed from the building. They fell on those already outside—Mad Hatter, Pigeon, and Henny Penny, chiefly. Henny cried, 'I'm getting smashed to bits!' She may not have been smashed, but she surely looked bad—singed, soaked, and screaming. All the residents had soaked feathers or fur, burned patches, and dents from tumbling out the building.

White Rabbit was running around and around the building. 'Pull the walls down! We have to get the fire out!'

Just as the last few inhabitants poured out the doors and down the stairs, the walls came down. Cascades of water, fire, desks, ducks, chickens, hares, and hatters flowed out. With the walls of the first, second, and third floors gone, the roof plopped down on the remains and sat on the basement. *Crash! Clatter! Clang! Kaboom! Crunch!*

'I'm in charge!' said White Rabbit. 'I saved the building!'

'Saved?! Saved?' Does he really think that?' asked Duck, shaking his wet feathers.

'White Rabbit makes his own reality,' said Goose, flapping water off his feet.

Mad Hatter and March Hare were drying off. 'Thank goodness we don't live here,' said Mad Hatter. 'It's bad enough we have an office in here.' She poured water out of her black fur hat.

'Bad is right,' said March Hare. 'It's almost time for tea. I'm going home.'

Alix hardly recognized Dragon Lady and Red Dean when they crawled out from under the roof. Red Dean was flat, altogether flat, without her air. She'd been punctured by Henny's escape ladder, it seemed. Dragon Lady was all claws and teeth and singed wings. The other birds had singed feathers and throbbing egos. Someone smelled like burnt rubber and sulfur dioxide. Most of the inhabitants had lost their offices and all their belongings, and since many of them lived in their offices, they were now without their nests and homes.

'Keep a stiff upper beak,' shouted Preying Praying Mantis down to them.

'Shut up!' several birds and animals shouted simultaneously back at her.

Preying Praying Mantis was dangling over a power line, her first three limbs on one side, the second three limbs on the other, with her stick body caught on the line. She had blown out of the building as it came down.

'Get her down,' shouted White Rabbit.

'Not yet!' shouted Slug, Drone, Duck, and Goose.

Alix felt sorry for the homeless birds and creatures. Most of them were crying. Several wandered aimlessly around. They now were even worse-looking than during the mud races, and worse smelling, something she had not thought was possible. They were used to following directions and now there were no directors directing. Red Dean was too winded to talk and Dragon Lady was still smoking.

The homeless inhabitants of Caedmon now had no homes, no offices, no dry clothes, and no sympathy from White Rabbit, who still insisted that he had saved everything. Even the chaotic mud races had been overseen by Red Dean and Dragon Lady, and everyone was now looking to them for answers to their lost offices and homes. But Red Dean was crawling around trying to retrieve her necklaces, and Dragon Lady was still trying to smother the smoking feathers on her wings.

Alix would have to call home. She had lost not only her jacket, hat, shoes, and her sweatshirt, but also her backpack containing Puppy, her money, and identification. She had no money, no extra clothes, no keys, and no morale. 'What'll I do?' she asked. 'My life washed away.'

She thought of how no one here knew her, how she had no identity. 'I could just as well find an ID and use it, and become another person. I might find some other clothes, with different names on them, and become somebody else. I don't even look like myself.'

Indeed, she didn't, with her usually curly hair now straight and darker, and her glasses gone. She had even lost her high school class ring while swimming.

Chapter Five

Advice from a Caterpillar

Alix felt cold. What clothes she still had were wet. In the ruins of Caedmon all of the offices from the second and third floors had dropped into the basement. Some animals were whimpering, some crying. She had never seen chickens cry before. Henny Penny was the worst, as usual. She said, 'They're trying to drown us. Everyone thinks I'm crazy, but they tried to drown us at the races, then they tried to drown us in Caedmon Hall.'

Preying Praying Mantis had fallen off the power line and now she looked like a bundle of sticks on the ground. Crab had moved off to the pond where he would be safer. So had Duck and Goose. 'We never should have moved inside,' Goose said. 'Caedmon was full of cracks and would have fallen sometime.'

Duck said, 'Remember when what's-his-name attached a caliper to the crack so he could keep a record as it widened? We knew this building was about to fall.'

Alix's advisor had sent instructions for her to meet with him now, and he was emphatic about the time, so she headed to the new building, Mazin Grates, which turned out to be a sprawling tan-colored building of one floor. Circling the building was an embankment and a stream of water, so Alix had to find a bridge. The water, bridge, and embankment reminded her of medieval castles she had visited. 'At least I won't have to go downstairs into dark corridors,' she said to herself, 'or get caught upstairs in a burning building, or downstairs in a flooding building.'

In the foyer Alix saw a directory and three glass boxes containing pictures of faculty. 'This will be helpful,' she said to herself. She found carefully labeled pictures of some of the faculty she had already met: Pigeon, Janus JekyllHyde, and White Rabbit.

Janus JekyllHyde's two images were in separate boxes, each picture showing a different face and different expression, and each was labeled. One picture was labeled Queen Margrethe of Denmark. 'When did she become a faculty member?' Alix asked. Then she saw another label below that one. It read, *'The woman in the picture above is not Queen Margrethe of Denmark, but Margaret Ankeny of Wayzata, a member of the Board of Regents.*

In the next case Alix saw the label Red Dean and looked closely at the picture. It did not at all resemble the person she had seen. Red Dean was very large and very red, but this photograph showed something even larger and not at all red. It was more angular, too. Red Dean was usually quite round. Then she saw that it had another label below the first, this one reading, 'The object in the picture has been misidentified. It does not show Red Dean, but the new water tower.'

Ostrich had arrived and was standing in the middle of the foyer addressing a group of prospective students. 'We will soon dedicate the new building. It has been open for the past few months, but the ceremony will give us an opportunity to reflect on its need—a void that has taken a long time in becoming a reality.'

Ostrich led the group into the hall behind him to show the students how each hall was color-coded, something like an airport terminal. The halls were named Tan Hall, Beige Hall, Mocha Hall, and Sand Hall. They fanned out from the foyer in different directions and each hallway began with a huge grate, a portcullis that dropped behind anyone who entered the hallway. Ostrich said, gesturing towards the grate, 'I like it. I really do. It combines a masculine feel of medieval strength with a delightful sense of play in the portcullis decorations.'

Each portcullis had a different design. The instructions from Alix's advisor said to walk under the portcullis with the battle-ax design and follow Tan Hall until the second branch, then turn left. She entered the hallway and jumped as the grate fell behind her. She hoped she wasn't trapped. The grate being very large and made of wrought iron, she'd never be able to budge it by herself. As she walked to the first turn she heard a voice from within an office, someone reading to another person: 'It was Saturday night. The clock on my office wall showed the time to be 11:45. There are times when a private eye does not necessarily feel like being a private eye. This was one of those times. The elevator door down the hall clanked open with a clank familiar to anyone on the fourth floor. Footsteps came down the darkened hall. They were the footsteps of a woman. . . .' Alix wondered if somehow the writer was recording her visit, except Mazin Grates had no elevator. She was thankful she wouldn't have to stay and hear the novel. It would probably go on forever, and at that pace.

She looked at the professor's nameplate on his desk: Ivan Ho. 'Well, at least he's not my advisor,' she said. She reached the corner and turned left into a maze of halls, none of them marked with numbers or names. All of them were some shade of tan. A meeting in progress attracted her attention because she could hear the chair saying, 'The big committee hasn't been able to do anything with this problem, the middle-sized committee hasn't been able to do anything with it, and the small committee hasn't been able to do anything. Following protocol, I suggest that we now forward it to the teensy-weensy committee.'

Alix checked her instructions from her advisor but couldn't find any direction about what to do after the first turn. She decided to turn left at every corner and hope for the best. 'If he said to turn left at the first corner, maybe I should turn left at all the other corners,' she said. 'I can't be sure I won't repeat myself, but if I keep turning left I'll know that to get out I have to take right turns.' All of the halls looked just alike. Some had open doors but none of the doors had names on them.

Alix heard another voice and looked into a classroom. A professor who looked like a crane was saying, 'We don't discover truth—we create it. Everything you know is wrong. Language uses us more than we use it. It gives you operating instructions for your four-dimensional, electrochemical, protoplasmic hologram, your brain. Analytic and non-analytic modes of thought . . .'

'No thank you,' said Alix. 'I'm totally confused by these endless tan halls. I don't need an endless tan lecture.' She walked toward two professors standing at the next corner. She hoped they might know her advisor. They were wearing baggy pants and sweatshirts, with their pens clipped to the tattered necks of the shirts. One was saying, 'All this has become possible because one of the happy paradoxes of computer technology is that as it grows in complexity of performance, it diminishes in simplicity of operation.'

The other blinked and leaned forward. 'I'm sorry. What were you saying? I must have dozed off for a second.'

Alix heard the grate at the last intersection of halls slam shut. A student from the orientation group, small and red-haired with a little girl's voice, was also trapped in the hall. She asked Alix, 'Have you visited these classes? Aren't they fascinating?'

Alix shrugged. 'Oh, they're interesting all right. They just don't happen to interest me.'

'I seem to need a serious challenge.' As the student spoke Alix heard more grates slamming down distant halls, the sounds echoing through the hallways so she couldn't tell where they had originated. Alix thought of her own serious challenges, of finding her advisor and finding a way through all the steel grates and out of this maze.

From a nearby hall came Ostrich's voice calling, 'Bill! Bill! Lizard Bill! You 're the only one who can fit through the grates and get the keys into the hall!'

White Rabbit appeared beside Ostrich. 'Why must we always depend upon Bill? We should burn all of these grates.'

'Burn?' said Ostrich. 'This is the new building.'

'Burn the grate down,' insisted White Rabbit. 'Destroy it to save the building.'

Alix wondered how iron was supposed to burn, and when White Rabbit would learn his lesson, and why they put everything on Bill. 'I wouldn't be in Bill's place for a good deal. If anything goes wrong . . .'

Bill soon came through the grate carrying a big key in his mouth and he unlocked the grate nearest Alix, just as he had unlocked all the others. 'What a maze!' exclaimed Alix. 'I thought I'd never find my way out.'

'You didn't,' said Bill. 'Follow me.' And he began leading Alix to her advisor's office.

Alix thought Lizard Bill looked familiar. 'Were you in the mud races?' she asked. 'I was never sure who was who, or who won.'

'Neither was I,' said Bill. 'I don't remember anything except someone hollering at me, then Red Dean saying I was the next Jewel in the Crown. I was bogged down in the mud. Some jewel. I thought I'd lost because someone was standing on me and I couldn't move. I gagged on mud.'

'Did you win?' Alix couldn't remember much from all that confusion. Where had Bill been?

'Red Dean grabbed me and put me in a chair so that I was sitting under a suspended steel ball. Then she said, "Remember, Bill, this is only a test," so I thought of it as a test. But that didn't stop me from turning white and wetting the chair. That turned out to be the real test, the steel ball test.'

'What happened next?' Alix and Bill had been walking for some time, turning more and more corners down identical halls until Alix was totally disoriented.

'Red Dean congratulated me on a successful race and test,' said Bill, 'but I don't know when I raced or where the finish was. I only know that somehow I was her winner.'

Bill was a winner, taking Alix right to her advisor's office at the end of the hall and opening a grate decorated with mushrooms and pipes, mostly Turkish water pipes.

'Here's your advisor, in the developing room. He's already developed from larva to pupa and he's only been at it seventeen years.'

Alix saw her advisor sitting on a mushroom smoking a hookah. She wasn't sure whether he was a caterpillar, or an inch worm, or another drone. He had arms and legs, so he wasn't a slug.

'I'm Alix,' she said, 'and I received your message that I was to meet you now.'

'So?' he puffed. 'Who are yooouuu?'

'Alix,' she repeated.

'Can you prove it?' Smoke rings swirled around his head.

'No. Not right now.'

'Well then, are you sure who you are?' He puffed on his hookah again.

Alix wanted to ask him who—or what—he was, but she thought he would resent it. He looked fierce, with eyes glazed over and the lower lids rising halfway up. She tried to remember whether she had heard there were poisonous worms anywhere. Caterpillar looked poisonous. 'You're my advisor and I'm supposed to meet with you. You sent me a message.'

'What is your major?' Caterpillar reached for a stack of blue books.

'I'm not sure yet,' she said.

'You aren't sure of much, are you?' Caterpillar took another puff of his pipe and pulled a blue book out of the stack.

'I'm sure that you sent me a message to meet with you.' Alix showed him the message.

'I called this meeting so I can learn some of the issues that are on my mind.' Blowing a smoke ring at her, he offered her a blue book. 'Is this your test?'

Attempting to turn his attention to his advising duties, Alix said, 'I've seen some of the classes. I visited several of them.' She thought of all the classes she had overheard from the hall, hoping he wouldn't ask her to name them. But then she decided he wouldn't remember anything she said anyway, since he obviously couldn't remember that she had only recently arrived on campus.

Caterpillar seemed to have forgotten why she was there. 'Did you see a woman in a pink flowered dress with a look of disgust on her face pass by?' He riffled through another stack of blue books, still trying to locate Alix's for her.

'No. Do I need to talk to her?' Alix hoped he would forget the blue books and advise her.

'Don't distract me. She's getting Lizard Bill,' said Caterpillar, blowing smoke rings at Alix.

Alix was confused. 'Why Lizard Bill? Why is she getting him?'

'Why are you here?' Some advisor, Alix thought. Who needs him? Caterpillar seemed disappointed that he had not found her blue book.

Alix blew smoke back at him. 'I'm no longer sure. I'm not sure why I bothered to come here at all.'

'Who are you?'

At that moment the woman in the flowered dress returned with Bill clutched in her hand. She had him grasped by the neck. 'Got him.'

'Good,' said Caterpillar. 'It's time for his training.'

Alix soon found out what the training was. The woman was Bill's faculty mentor, charged with developing him, filling him out into tenure shape. She poured some blue ooze down his throat until he changed colors, first blue, then purple, then green, then orange.

'Done,' said Caterpillar. 'Are you sure he's the right one? Did Red Dean select him? Maybe we should check with her again. Did you pour all the ooze down his throat?' Alix noticed that Caterpillar always seemed to be unsure of what he had just heard. Maybe it was all the smoke making him dizzy.

'Good,' said Caterpillar. 'He's the right one. That was easy. Now he's a chameleon.' He now seemed unsure of what he had just said.

'He has to be to survive,' said the woman, who had begun to resemble a turtle. Her back curved to meet her head, her neck disappeared, and her head sank into her back. The pink flowers on her dress seemed to be fading into sea green and muddy gray. Alix thought that she too must also be a chameleon.

'Next, do his eyes,' said the turtle woman. Alix saw that she suddenly seemed to have a shell instead of a dress.

The two of them, Caterpillar and Turtle Woman, strangled Lizard Bill until his eyes popped out and began rotating independently.

'Now he can see all sides,' said Turtle as she stretched her head out for a moment to see all sides.

'And watch his behind,' said Caterpillar, releasing Bill, who turned to look behind himself.

Turtle said, 'Reptiles are the easiest to work with, snakes and lizards especially, because they already have forked tongues. We don't have to split them.'

'So many of the faculty object when we split their tongues,' sighed Caterpillar. 'If only they knew we're doing them a favor. They'll need bifurcated tongues.' Both tips of his tongue licked his lips, one tip licking the upper lip, one the lower.

'They behave like chickens!' exclaimed Turtle, safe in her shell.

'Of course, many are chickens to begin with,' commented Caterpillar. 'Do you think Bill would be better off as a chicken?' He reached for his pipe.

'We just agreed that reptiles have more advantages,' said Turtle. 'For one thing, they are naturally cold-blooded, so we don't have to freeze them. That makes promotion easier on them.'

Then she looked at Bill, who was turning from orange to blue. 'Look, he's turning blue on his own. I think he's done.' She released Bill. 'I've never had a cat make the transition yet. They enjoy their warm pads too much. Plus, they're too independent-minded to read Red Dean's E-mail messages, no matter how often they are told to read and respond daily.'

'Just too uncooperative,' agreed Caterpillar. 'I'm not surprised that Red Dean removed all of them. "Why borrow trouble?" as she always says. We have so many totally uncooperative faculty. Some of them only cooperate when they are coerced. Forced to volunteer, as it were.'

Turtle nodded. 'Bill's all set physically. Now for the essential qualities.' She looked at several bottles and a funnel on the shelf. The two of them recaptured Bill and forced open his mouth. They selected the bottles labeled

Certainty and Confidence. Caterpillar also picked up those labeled Credibility and Infallibility.

The door burst open. Dragon Lady had arrived to supervise. 'Remember when all the institution needed was a little fine tuning? Now we have to have these conversion sessions after the races for tenure.' She herself had converted into a gargoyle, with large features, especially her lips and nose, stiff flared wings and ears, and pointed teeth. Alix couldn't decide which Dragon Lady was more frightening, the dragon with thin lips and folded wings, or the gargoyle with thick lips and stiff wings. She was glad she didn't need converting into something. Seeing Lizard Bill change from a lizard into a horned toad was scary enough.

Turtle Woman felt Bill's sides. 'His toad bumps are coming out. He'll need those while his skin thickens.'

'Out of sight!' Dragon Lady then observed Turtle's shell. 'I see you've grown a good thick shell. Red Dean's skin has thinned. It became elastic first, then very thin.' She spread her elastic wings out.

'Well, her responsibilities have grown tremendously, and so has she,' said Caterpillar.

'Now she's the big enchilada for sure,' added Dragon Lady.

'No one says 'big enchilada' any more.' Turtle released her grip on Bill and he fell down. He was now bumpy and purple, with gold highlights.

'Get with it,' said Dragon Lady, 'I think it's groovy.' She turned to Bill. 'Here's a little tip, Bill. Try to be more like me.' She stood up very straight and folded her wings, becoming a black column.

'Has he administrator potential?' asked Turtle.

'I thought that Lizard Bill ignored his evaluations, and held himself unaccountable,' said Caterpillar as he puffed his hookah again. Stinky blue smoke filled the room.

'That's what makes him management material, according to Red Dean,' said Dragon Lady. 'He's thirty-seven now, reads his E-mail every day and responds. She says that by forty-five, usually all the bugs are worked out, but Bill learned sooner than most.'

'I am changing soon into a moth,' said Caterpillar. 'That's safer than remaining a bug.'

'What do you think moths are, if not bugs?' Dragon Lady asked, eyes blazing, wings flaring. She had blazed all over during the fire, but now only her eyes burned. She was once again tall and angular with long filmy black clothes and big hair.

Bill shook himself. 'Am I done? I'm going to go out there and play like I've never played before.' His eyes rotated, one clockwise, one counterclockwise.

'Teach, Bill, teach. Not play,' said Caterpillar. 'Did we get the right Bill?' He puffed his pipe. 'I don't know about this Bill.' Caterpillar seemed able to contradict himself more than Janus's two faces.

'All set up to get up on the stump?' asked Turtle, ignoring Caterpillar's doubts. He always doubted everything, even his own actions and words.

'I'm a lizard, not a frog,' said Bill, flicking his tail and running up and down the hallway.

'Oh, yes, so you are,' said Turtle. 'Your body is so nice and round now with the Qualities we poured in, I thought you were a frog. You're almost as good as a turtle.'

'I can be a frog! I'll change!' cried Bill.

'It worked! He can change,' said Caterpillar.

'Here's your tenure certificate, Bill,' said Dragon Lady. 'The committee will ratify and send you confirmation next month.' Alix wondered if they had forgotten she was listening to all of this. Red Dean had controlled the races, the outcomes, the rewards, and now Dragon Lady had orders to reconstruct Bill and give him tenure. Alix had once wondered who had the power in this institution, but now it was obvious. Red Dean sent E-mail messages several times a day and logged in all responses. All of the chaos was a diversion to confuse the faculty. Turkey Lurkey seemed to understand this, and he tried to cozy up to her power. Dragon Lady certainly understood this, and she tried to align herself with power, not always successfully. Some other faculty members seemed to believe they would be judged on their merits, when in fact they were judged on their adherence to Red Dean's orders. Alix wondered how it related to learning, to the ideals of the Institution— to Love, or Fairness, or Freedom or Autonomy. None of these ideals had anything to do with power. The happier faculty—Goose, Duck, Slug, Drone, Mad Hatter, and March Hare—ignored the power struggles, did their work, and avoided Red Dean. She might never reward or praise them for their success in publishing, but they found rewards outside the Institution, among their peers.

Alix wished she could swallow some identity and feel herself again. She was still without her sweatshirt, shoes, and jacket. Her feet were cold. 'I always thought "cold feet" was just an expression,' she said to herself as she followed Bill out of the building. Just outside she came upon Mad Hatter and March Hare sitting on their motorized tea cart, drinking tea and offering some to everyone around them. Their teapot was a miniature Japanese pagoda, complete with gongs to summon guests, tiny benches, and ceramic flowers, all brightly painted. They had packed their laptop computers into the tea cart and changed into different dresses. March Hare's was a long deep pink skirt, a white blouse with pansies embroidered all over, and Mad Hatter wore a cocktail dress of bright red tulle, a hat of red feathers framing her face, and red shoes and purse. They had dressed up more than usual to draw attention to Mad Hatter's new song, which Goose accompanied on a guitar.

Tale of a Tenure, or Songs of Tenure Chasing

She thought she went to graduate school
To learn the rule of three,
But then she found, to her surprise
She learned the rule of me.
She thought she saw an Oxford don
Expatiate in Greek,
But then she found, to her surprise
A don too dumb to speak.
She thought she learned her Derrida
To write in MLA,
But then she found, to her surprise,
The Frog had had his day.
O sing a song of tenure,
A pocketful of rye,
Fifty assistant professors
Baked until they die.

Chapter Six

Invitation to a Match

Alix was grateful to Bill for helping her escape the maze. She saw a fish, or what looked like a fish, wearing a white wig and a dress coat, walking—sort of—towards a house at the edge of the campus. He moved by twisting his body from side to side, alternating the tips of his tail fins on the ground. He had no trouble breathing, though. He might be a fish out of water, but he had adjusted remarkably well to air.

The house seemed to be made of cement blocks, with tiny windows, no shutters, no paint, no shrubbery in the front. It resembled a bunker, or a jail from the Old West. The fish rang the doorbell, a set of chimes with three live, squid-shaped gargoyles on the crosspiece. Each faced a different direction, seemingly guarding the door, which had a nameplate held in place by a larger, more frightening gargoyle, who snarled as Alix read the nameplate: Dragon Lady. A frog in a white wig, morning coat, gray trousers, and starched shirt, answered 'Yes? Who calls?'

'Forgive me for coming in person,' said the fish, 'but our computers are down.' He stood up on his tail fin. 'I'm delivering a summons—uh, invitation to Red Dean's croquet match.'

The frog stood up as straight as frog legs could. 'Hasn't the Red Holiness learned to use E-mail yet?' As he spoke, he adjusted his bow tie and stiff shirtfront.

'No, she hasn't. But that's not the problem,' said Fish. 'Our computers are down.'

'We use E-mail all the time,' said Frog. 'We can send orders much faster this way.'

'E-mail! She can't even turn on her computer! I have to download everything for her.' Fish gulped for air. He seemed to be drowning in work.

'Dragon Lady uses E-mail as a weapon,' said Frog. 'You should be grateful Red Dean hasn't learned electronic ordinance yet.'

'So this is Dragon Lady's house,' said Alix. 'At least it doesn't look big enough for me to get lost in.' She decided to follow Frog into Dragon Lady's house because she could smell food cooking and her hunger overcame her dread of Dragon Lady. 'I'd better get used to Dragon Lady. She seems to be Red Dean's chief assistant.'

Fish said, 'It sounds good, probably, when I say that Red Dean can't use E-mail, but she makes me do it for her. I sent 378 messages yesterday, printed 176, and organized the messages by the sender's rank and size.'

'Size? Size of what?' asked Frog. He put his hands up to his eyes as though to measure their size.

'Size of office. The bigger the office, the earlier she reads the message.' Fish enjoyed jolting the staff members who were already frightened and seeing them jump some more.

Frog stretched his fingers. 'Did you work late? Doing all the E-mail?'

'Late? I haven't slept in weeks, and haven't eaten. That's why she hired a fish, so I wouldn't have to stop and eat or sleep. Luckily I grew some fingers.'

'I'd noticed you have fingers now,' said Frog as he stretched his own fingers again.

'Red Dean said I'd have to develop fingers or she'd feed me to the alligators.' Fish flexed his fangangs, his word for fingers.

Alix was beginning to think she was better off as a student. She might have lost her clothes and ID, but she didn't have to change color, or species, or shape, or grow fingers or a round body, as Fish and Lizard Bill were doing. She thought of some of the faculty members who tried to please Red Dean in order to receive a grant. Fish and Frog were no worse off than they were.

Frog performed a few squat-thrusts as Fish adjusted his wig. "My hair works hard, and it plays hard,' said Fish. He looked around for a window so he could see how his wig sat.

'Your hair is a wig!' exclaimed Frog. 'Have you for-gotten?'

'So, what's your point?' Fish found his reflection in the window. 'The custom in our family was to bind the heads of infants to make them look like Chinook salmon.'

'The custom in our family is to eat small fish. Fish, shrimp, prawns, prongs. All delicious,' commented Frog, licking his mouth, eyes, and the top of his head, as frogs do.

Fish jumped back, adjusted his wig one more time, and left, so Alix followed Frog into Dragon Lady's kitchen. Dragon Lady was stirring a big pot from which steam was rising. It filled the room, making the kitchen warm and humid.

'Stew?' asked Alix. It smelled like a seafood gumbo, but one with cabbage.

'Slew,' said Dragon Lady. Since escaping the fire and flood of Caedmon Hall, she had recovered her dragon shape and had also recovered her blazing expression and disposition. Now that she was home among her gargoyles, she no longer resembled a gargoyle herself. On her apron was a Jolly Roger, and her chef's hat, black rather than white, was pinned in the classic pirate shape. Her knife looked like a machete. She reminded Alix of the Dragon Lady in *Terry and the Pirates.* Maybe that's where she comes from, thought Alix, and she stood as far away from her as she could.

Dragon Lady was holding a screaming baby as she stirred the steaming pot. The howls added to the tense ambiance of the kitchen, which smelled of cooked cabbage and turnips. 'Bummer,' she said.

'Is this your baby?' asked Alix, leaning over and trying to see its face.

'No one owns children,' said Dragon Lady as she threw some shrimp into the pot.

Alix tried again. 'Are you the baby's mother?' She'd seen that the baby was totally bald.

'No one knows. The stork stopped here and left it under a cabbage leaf. I picked it up but I don't have to like it.' Dragon Lady peered into her pot. Steam and the smell of cabbage filled the room, competing for air space with the howling baby. Alix's ears and nose hurt.

Alix thought of Eleanor, who had picked her up and had liked her. She also thought of her little sister Lily, whom she had cared for as a baby. She thought of her cats Dinah and Cheshire, whom she was always picking up. She wondered where they all were. Alix and Eleanor had arrived on campus together, but since the assembly Alix was alone. She had been lost in dark corridors, in a burning and flooding building, in a mud race, and in a mazy building, and now she found herself in a dragon's kitchen watching her cook who knows whom.

Dragon Lady began throwing the baby into a somer-
sault over her head, catching it just before it fell into the
pot, and hollering, 'Cool it!' at the baby when it screamed
more. Finally she threw it at Alix. 'Heads up! Catch!
Catch it!'

'Do you want me to care for it?' asked Alix, catching
the baby and cuddling it.

'It's as much yours as mine. Besides, I have to stir my
slew.' She peered into the steam rising from the pot and
said, 'I should have grabbed that fish messenger.'

Alix said, 'Do you mean to put him into your pot?'

Dragon Lady turned to glare at her. 'If everybody
minded their own business, the world would go around
a great deal faster than it does.' She flapped her wings to
clear the steam. 'Now that we're friends with China, I
could go for some Moo Goo Gai Pan and a side order of
ribs.'

That didn't make much sense to Alix, but then nothing else did either. She wondered whose ribs. Alix handed
Dragon Lady the invitation from Red Dean, thinking she
was safer than the fish footman, then saw that Dragon
Lady was eating a fish that still had its head on and was
drinking red wine in great gulps. The fish's eyes looked
alive. Dragon Lady was agitated—even more than usual
—by the invitation from Red Dean. 'I've got to fly. All faculty must be summoned and now I have to do it alone.
Red Dean's E-mail is out. I have to gather all the equipment.' She began throwing croquet mallets and balls and
hoops towards Alix.

Alix was still holding the baby. 'Stop! The baby will
get hurt!' Its cries tormented her.

'No way, José. Babies don't get hurt unless you mean
to hurt them.' Dragon Lady threw some more mallets.
'Shut up and help me.'

'Babies are our future! Stop!' Alix caught some of the
mallets and dodged some others.

'Don't be so sentimental about the future!' said Dragon Lady, 'I think of the past. I do so miss the food in Lucerne. In Khartoum! In Shanghai!'

Alix thought the baby was beginning to resemble a squid, and she hoped Dragon Lady wouldn't notice—she might want to steam it for the slew. Meanwhile, Dragon Lady had turned back to the pot. 'Mmmmmmm. The soup du jour is not cream of mushroom. It is not tomato or celery. It is not chicken, nor is it Scotch broth. It is most definitely not wonton. . . . What should I call it?' Alix smelled turnips, cabbage, fish, shrimp, but she was too afraid of Dragon Lady to suggest any name.

Alix definitely did not want to stay and taste the soup because she thought it might contain someone she knew, so she slipped out the back door and went over toward a stone fence, where she thought she saw a striped cat. But she saw that it was really two cats, the same colors as her own cats, Dinah and Cheshire, one all white and one striped gray and gold. A cat gargoyle with a planter in its back perched on the fence also. Unlike the live gargoyle on the front door, this was clearly a stone statue. Farther down the fence was another cat statue, this time a round brown Buddha-shaped cat with a smile of contentment. As Alix approached the fence, she saw Cheshire's face appear, or was it the original Cheshire Cat? Whoever it was, she was glad to see her. Or him. 'At last! This is too scary for a dream. And too long.' Alix was terrified of Dragon Lady, tired from the maze, still damp from swimming, and now dizzy with hunger and scared for the baby.

Alix asked Cheshire, 'Can you talk?'

'What do you think?' asked the cat, sitting up to wash its face.

'Can you help me?' asked Alix, who could now see that this cat was indeed the Cheshire Cat, for his tail had disappeared. Besides, he talked!

'What sort of help?' asked the cat, who was proving to be just as puzzling to her as he was to Alice. Now an ear vanished. Alix hoped his mouth wouldn't vanish before he talked to her.

'Can you tell me what to do?' asked Alix, surprised that she would need advice from a cat.

'What do you want to do?' asked the cat. He looked behind himself at Dinah creeping up on him. His tail re-appeared and thrashed in excitement.

'What should I do with this baby?' asked Alix, noticing that Dinah was preparing to spring on the Cheshire Cat.

'What do you think you should do?' asked the cat. Dinah was creeping closer, and Alix considered whether she should warn the Cheshire Cat to turn around.

'Are you really trying to help me?' asked Alix, still wondering whether to warn Cheshire. She had often seen Dinah and her Cheshire play *kill* for hours at a time, and usually one of them got scratched.

'What do you think?' asked the cat, seeming to sense Dinah, and turning suddenly to face her. His fur stood up at least fourteen inches along his back and his tail became the size of an umbrella.

'I'll have to keep it for now,' said Alix. 'Where should I go?' She saw Cheshire had turned around so fast that Dinah jumped straight into the air, then flipped backwards.

'Where do you want to get to?' asked the cat as Dinah fell backwards off the stone wall and into a rose bush. They could hear her thrashing and uttering cat curses.

'Dragon Lady is going to the match. Maybe I'll go there,' said Alix, wondering where Dinah had fallen. Dinah's thrashes subsided but her curses didn't.

'Do you know where that is?' asked the cat, ignoring Dinah, who had quieted down for the moment.

'At Red Dean's house, I suppose,' said Alix. 'Where is that?' Alix approached the wall so she could peep over at Dinah reemerging from the rose bush.

'Do you know where Mad Hatter lives?' asked the cat, peering down at Dinah. One back foot and one front foot disappeared.

'I see a sign over there. Mad Hatter's Hut. Is that it?' asked Alix, pointing towards the sign. She would have to get over the fence and cross a stream to get there.

'What do you think?' asked the cat as he prepared to leap on Dinah, but couldn't without his back foot.

'Why aren't you more help?' asked Alix, scraping a stick on the wall to warn Dinah.

'How could I be?' asked the cat, now assuming the classic 'attack cat' crouch as his feet reappeared.

'You might try answering with a statement instead of a question,' said Alix. She saw that Dinah was now stalking a moth.

'How would that help?' asked the cat, creeping forward as Dinah followed the moth.

'Then I could learn something,' said Alix. Dinah leaped and grabbed the moth with both paws.

'And miss learning it for yourself?' asked the cat as he leaped at Dinah.

'Where's Red Dean's house?' asked Alix. She hoped he would let Dinah go while pointing out the direction of Red Dean's croquet field.

'Have you met March Hare?' asked the cat. He was rolling around and around in the grass with Dinah, thrashing his reappeared tail vigorously.

'What does that have to do with it?' asked Alix. 'Be serious for a moment.' Cheshire was serious about pinning Dinah down. His tail continued to thrash the ground in excitement.

'Where would that get you?' asked the cat as Dinah escaped and ran for a tree.

'Does March Hare live in that house with furry rabbit ears sticking out of the roof?' Alix watched Dinah leap ten feet up the tree trunk and scramble for the biggest branch.

'Is that the house of a person or a March Hare?' asked the cat. He leaped after Dinah but from too far away and missed the tree trunk altogether.

'I suppose no one would live in a house with rabbit ears.' Alix saw that he was embarrassed, as he paused to wash his ears and face.

'One might! We're all mad here!' said the cat. Alix decided he was both mad-crazy *and* mad-angry.

'A statement! I was beginning to think you were crazy.' The cat was now pretending that his jump was just a practice leap across the grass, not an attempt to catch Dinah, for he ignored Dinah.

'In this institution you have to be crazy,' said the cat, leaping back onto the stone wall, where he sat beside another cat gargoyle, this one sitting upright, with flared wings, teeth, and claws.

'Is this a mental institution?' asked Alix. She couldn't remember the name of the campus, or where it was located, and just now she couldn't remember where her backpack had been lost.

'Brains are our business!' said the cat. 'Enough small talk. Let's discuss money. Here's a package from your mother.'

The package contained Eleanor's own sweatshirt and windbreaker. Alix recognized the sweatshirt she had given Eleanor, embossed Genuine Antique Person, *made the old-fashioned way.* Alix put on the sweatshirt and jacket. 'What a relief to be warm again,' she said as she unpacked Eleanor's favorite Oriole baseball cap and put it on. 'Even better. Now I'm ready for the match, or whatever comes next.' She was relieved to see items from home, from normal people, things that would combat the madness and meanness and chaos of this place. Cheshire Cat was right about one thing: she was better off learning things for herself, not listening to the authorities.

Chapter Seven

A Mad Tea Party

Alix remembered that March Hare and Mad Hatter had a continuous tea party in *Alice in Wonderland*, and since she could not remember when she had last eaten, she hurried to the house with the furry rabbit ears on the roof. The house itself was not furry but white brick, more like a thatched-roofed cottage from the Cotswolds, surrounded by a flower garden of petunias, pansies, lilies, marigolds, and roses. Seeing a large table through the dining room window, Alix let herself in.

The table was set for twenty, for no one wanted to pause and clear it, and who knows who might show up? March Hare and Mad Hatter were indeed having tea and snacks. Alix looked around for a cradle for the baby, found one under a bay window, and slipped the baby into it.

March Hare asked, 'Who are you?'

'Alix,' said Alix. She edged closer to the table to see what food was being served.

'Can you prove it?' asked Mad Hatter as she rose from her place and took another. As she changed places, she also changed hats, from a deep gold cloche to a straw hat covered with daisies, and among the daisies a large green bird. Her dress was a simple knee-length royal blue cocktail dress with a sequined bodice. She wore a tiny white apron decorated with muffins, real muffins, which she ate from time to time.

'No,' said Alix, wondering if she would be as difficult as Caterpillar had been. She saw an empty chair between Mad Hatter and March Hare.

'Neither of us can prove who we are,' said Mad Hatter, 'so they call us mad.' She helped herself to a scone and some marmalade. She also fed the bird on her hat, giving it crumbs. Alix thought that of everyone she had met so far, these two might be bizarre, but not as mad as most.

'Who's your child?' asked March Hare, pushing aside her used plate and taking another.

'Dragon Lady gave it to me. I think it's hers,' said Alix, slipping into the chair between them. At least they weren't cooking anyone she knew. They had desserts, lots of desserts.

'Beware of Dragons bearing gifts,' said Mad Hatter, pouring tea for herself.

'Can we have some tea now?' asked Alix. 'I'm done in.' Smelling the tea and scones was making her ravenous.

'Done in what?' asked March Hare, looking into a teapot shaped like a cottage with at least twelve ceramic kittens perched on the handle, the spout, the lid, and the ledge of grass and flowers around it. March Hare's apron had a design of psychedelic-colored shrimp, crabs, and lobsters. She wore a tall, puffy, pink chef's hat.

'Done in a minute!' said Mad Hatter, pouring tea for March Hare and Alix.

'Done in a hurry!' said March Hare. She searched for the sandwiches.

'Done in. Tired. Hungry,' said Alix. 'I've been lost in a catacomb, caught in a burning building, almost drowned, lost in a maze—'

'You're careless, aren't you?' asked Mad Hatter. 'You keep losing yourself.' Mad Hatter found another plate of scones, perched on a nearby chair.

'I lost my clothes, too,' said Alix. 'I lost some in the cave and the rest in the flood.' She hoped they would soon find some sandwiches.

'You are careless,' said March Hare. 'First you lost yourself, then your clothes.' She found another plate on another unoccupied chair, this time a plate of boiled corn-on-the-cob.

Alix felt defeated again. 'Why are you so rude? I lost my clothes in Windy Hole.' She began drooling at the sight of the corn.

Mad Hatter said, 'Have you lost your plans? You have clothes now. Are you always going to be so difficult?' She buttered an ear of corn and began eating, one row at a time.

March Hare poured some tea and ate a salad. 'This visitor is completely fictitious but extremely well written.'

'How can you say I'm fictitious?' asked Alix. She was hungrier than ever, thirsty, and exasperated. The smell of the corn made her hungrier and hungrier.

Mad Hatter said, 'Easy. You lost your name.' She finished the corn and took another.

'I did not lose my name,' said Alix. 'I lost my ID.' Alix didn't want to mention the whole backpack she'd lost, since it was one more proof of her incompetence as far as they were concerned. As Mad Hatter munched her corn, Alix winced. When would they offer her some?

'Same thing. Now you'll tell me you forgot why you came,' said March Hare. She remembered a cherry pie and got it from the pie safe.

'I came here to visit classes, but I got lost in the dark,' said Alix. Somehow the dark also seemed to be inside her. She felt hungry and out of sorts, even among these hospitable women. At least they weren't ordering people about, as so many others were.

'Aha! See? You're lost—lost—lost!' Mad Hatter took the pie and cut a slice. It smelled like apple pie but it was as dark as blueberry. Maybe they had combined the fruit.

'This is what we mean by significant deterioration,' said March Hare, looking at the rapidly vanishing corn and pie. But Alix thought March Hare was probably referring to her—Alix—and her alleged carelessness. Alix certainly felt deteriorated in body and spirit.

Alix now was not only hungry but getting dizzy from turning her head from side to side as Mad Hatter and March Hare spoke from either side of her. She was relieved to see others arriving for the party. White Rabbit and Turkey Lurkey sat down across the table from her, tossing aside a furry head from Mad Hatter's stuffed animal collection and helping themselves to scones and tea.

'Be careful with that!' said Mad Hatter. 'That might be somebody's little mother!' She now removed the daisy hat, replacing it with a gold sombrero, stylishly decorated with little pots of live herbs—rosemary, thyme, lavender, and oregano—perched on the big brim.

'Did you ever know one of those days when you thought you'd never be soft and fluffy again?' asked White Rabbit. He was looking at the little furry head, but his own fur was stiff and matted, not only his head fur, but also his hands, feet, arms, legs, tail, everything. He'd gotten too close to the fire, too close to the flood.

Alix, who had not seen White Rabbit since the she'd been trapped in Mazin Grates, asked, 'Is everyone at Caedmon safe? Everyone who was in Caedmon?' White Rabbit was checking his bow tie and plaid vest in the large mirror in the dining room, then dabbing at his stiff fur with a brush.

'There's the slightest chance that someone may have been killed, but I saved the building,' said White Rabbit. He seemed pleased with his reflection of perfection.

'How can you say that?' asked Alix. 'Everything above the basement was burned.'

'Not the roof. The roof and the basement are fine. I saw to that.' White Rabbit smiled at his reflection. His neat clothes reflected his peace of mind.

'The basement is flooded!' exclaimed Alix. The plate of scones was finally within reach, but she was too stunned by White Rabbit's statement to take one. How could White Rabbit think he'd saved Caedmon? How could he possibly believe what he was saying?

'I was in command,' said White Rabbit. 'Everything was taken care of.'

'What about all the computers in the basement?' asked Alix. 'What about all the offices and homes that fell into the basement?'

'I made plans for everyone. No one has ever accused me of being stupid,' said White Rabbit, brushing a speck of lint off his bow tie.

'Truly, this is a tale told by an idiot,' said Mad Hatter, passing the plate of scones around. She replaced her sombrero with a dunce cap, striped purple, pink, orange, and yellow.

'Will the classes be moved to other buildings?' asked Alix, watching the scones as the plate went around the table, unfortunately in the other direction, away from her.

'I've saved the building, haven't I?' asked White Rabbit, taking one of the last few scones. 'I have pictures to prove it,' insisted White Rabbit, pulling out his photos.

'And they call us mad,' said Mad Hatter. 'This reminds me of *The Emperor's New Clothes*. No one can tell the emperor that his clothes are nonexistent. No one can tell White Rabbit that his walls are gone. He thinks he can make something exist by insisting it exists.'

'He's clearly mad,' said Alix.

Turkey Lurkey finished his scone. 'We're all mad about teaching.' His jowls flapped.

Alix took a scone before the platter disappeared. 'I expected a mad tea party, but not this mad.'

'We couldn't get any mad-tea.' Mad Hatter shook the teapot but found it empty.

'We had to get sad-tea,' said March Hare. 'A sad story.'

'Here,' said Mad Hatter, 'put Turkey Lurkey into the teapot. He has flavor, even if it's bad.'

'Bad-tea!' cried March Hare. 'A new sensation.'

Turkey Lurkey puffed his chest out. 'I am not one of those people who are easily offended.

'Ho ho!' chortled Mad Hatter, exchanging her dunce cap for a red pillbox with a veil.

'Was that funny?' asked Turkey Lurkey. 'I think I deserve an apology from Mad Hatter.' He stood on his chair and looked down at Mad Hatter, who was looking for a purse to match her new red hat.

'I do not know precisely what happened, but I think my noble friend deserves an apology,' said White Rabbit.

'Who did it?' asked Mad Hatter, giving Alix some tea and another scone.

'An apology has been asked for. It seems that none of us was quite clear what happened to cause my noble friend to seek an apology, but if a noble turkey asks for an apology for some sort of uncouth interruption in your grace's tea party, he is entitled to one,' said White Rabbit.

'Hear! Hear!' said March Hare, who was coming in from the kitchen, and who obviously had not heard White Rabbit's pompous speech but wanted to shut him up. She carried a large teapot shaped like Cinderella's pumpkin-carriage, complete with gold scrollwork on the handle, lid, and sides, an ornate spout, and a porcelain Cinderella seated half inside, half outside, with her dress flowing down the side of the carriage. It held much more tea than the cottage teapot.

'I hear. I suggest that in the interest of the tea party, some sort of gesture from the host is required. Nobody wants to make a fuss over this.' White Rabbit looked at the others as he felt his coattails for the pocket with the handkerchief.

'Would Mad Hatter, out of her usual courtesy, make an apology?' asked March Hare.

'All I did was snort when Turkey Lurkey made a funny remark,' said Mad Hatter.

'I never make funny remarks,' said Turkey Lurkey, meaning to sit, but missing his chair and falling on the floor. His contacts lenses were diagonal again.

'And I never apologize,' said Mad Hatter, dropping more tea and boiling water into the teapot, then shaking it vigorously to mix everything. A few drops of hot water splashed on Turkey.

'She didn't mean to snort when you didn't mean to make a funny remark,' said March Hare, looking at Mad Hatter and trying to maintain a severe face.

'You're just as tacky but a tad less harebrained,' said Turkey Lurkey, now rising from the floor and sitting in the chair, his head tilting so far over that he almost missed the chair again.

Janus JekyllHyde arrived and sat at the end of the table. He read the menu. 'A pig's foot and a bottle of beer? That's what you're serving?' His round face frowned with annoyance.

Mad Hatter said, 'Omelets are our specialty. We have a system for mixing chemicals to make plastics, so our omelets are fat-free.'

Janus JekyllHyde said, 'Just give me some nice ice-cake.' His lean, sleepy face read the menu listing *Ice-Cake* and wanted to try it.

March Hare picked up the cake knife and began slicing pieces. 'How many slices? Lots? Scads? Umpteen?'

'Can you cut it a bit thinner than umpteen?' said Mad Hatter, handing the slice to Janus. She had changed into an emerald green garden-party dress covered with ruffles. Her hat was huge, green, and trimmed with peacock feathers.

'That's marvelous. I'll be thrilled,' said Janus Jekyll-Hyde's lean face.

'With my usual reservations, of course,' said his round face, spinning to the front to see the cake.

'Do you like the cake?' asked March Hare. 'It's full of veggies. We named it Veggie Delight!'

'Yes, veggies, everyone must eat veggies at every meal,' said Janus JekyllHyde. 'I've named a campus Dieter to oversee this. He will have a staff of Dietacticians. Everything will be determined by the new Il Duce of Diet.' His round face beamed, his mustache twitched, he smiled.

'Who will that be?' asked White Rabbit. 'I'm good at control.' He dressed to give this impression, with his tightly buttoned plaid vest, neat bow tie, and small derby.

'I need a turkey I can trust,' said Janus JekyllHyde's lean face.

'So you've chosen Turkey Lurkey?' asked White Rabbit, his whiskers and hands twitching.

'Where did you hear that?' demanded Janus Jekyll-Hyde's power face. 'I'll find out who's responsible for this leak.' This face never looked sleepy. Never ever.

'You just said it,' said White Rabbit. 'You said you wanted a turkey you could trust. That means you've chosen Turkey Lurkey.'

'You are mistaken,' said Janus JekyllHyde. 'I said no such thing. Why are you always so contrary? Where did you hear that leak? I'll punish the leaker.'

Alix watched closely to see which face was really in control. Janus loved power and was willing to do anything, say anything, to ally himself with Red Dean, even if it meant shutting out his own face. He wanted to demonstrate iron control, Alix thought.

White Rabbit hid behind March Hare. Both were eating carrots and celery. Janus JekyllHyde's thin face glared at them. 'Why are you two always eating that rabbit food? How will you ever get strong? How do you think you rate, on a scale of one to ten?'

'Rate what?' asked March Hare.

'Besides, we are rabbits' chimed White Rabbit. 'Why wouldn't we eat rabbit food?'

'Fitness, of course,' said Janus JekyllHyde. 'What else is important?' His thin face did look fit, especially when compared with the round, frowning face.

'Didn't he just tell us that we had to eat veggies at every meal?' asked White Rabbit, still hiding behind March Hare.

'Janus changes,' said March Hare, 'according to which face has the forward position.'

'Just what is his role in the administration?' asked Alix. 'He seems so erratic, so mad—I mean angry.' She thought Mad Hatter might be sensitive to the word mad.

'I know he's in the campus community, but his role in it remains something of a mystery. He's a No/Yes man— No to his subordinates, Yes to his superordinates,' replied Mad Hatter. 'I know he's pretty mediocre, but on the other hand, we live in an age of mediocrity.' She served Janus some brussels sprouts and cabbage.

'It's the one indulgence he allows himself,' added March Hare, 'accepting his own mediocrity. He's completely pleased with himself.'

'Well,' said Mad Hatter, 'that was our farewell dinner. We're going to say goodbye to fresh garden vegetables.' She reached for a blueberry pie cooling on the buffet table.

When the phone rang March Hare pushed her chef's hat back to answer it, then said, 'It's Red Dean. She wants us at the croquet match.' She sliced the pie and gave Alix two pieces.

Tasting a slice of pie, Alix asked, 'Has she recovered from the fire?'

'She's completely puffed up again,' said March Hare. 'Nothing changed when her body flattened, except her body flattened.' She passed another platter full of scones around the table. Alix had finally met someone who ignored Red Dean's E-mail and phone messages.

'Now she's full of hot air again,' said Mad Hatter. 'As good as old.' She gave the plate of scones and a serving dish of marmalade to Alix.

'As good as new, you mean?' asked Alix. Now that she had the plate of scones, she kept it and ate several, with lots of marmalade.

'No! She's as good as old. She never changes.' Mad Hatter changed seats and hats again, this time into an orange hat with a wide brim full of berries.

'Especially her mind,' agreed March Hare. 'Her grudges are eternal.' March Hare threw away her old plate and took a clean one from the china cabinet. Who else on the faculty could eat so calmly after a call from Red Dean, Alix wondered. She saw that Mad Hatter had not only turned off, but also unplugged the computer.

'She blames White Rabbit for the fire,' said Turkey Lurkey, turning to glare at White Rabbit. He also blamed White Rabbit for the fire, Alix thought. Turkey automatically ingratiated himself with Red Dean; by adopting all her attitudes and grudges and by carefully reading and logging in her E-mail directives, he never had to decide whom to follow, but simply followed the power source.

'Red Dean spread it!' shouted White Rabbit. 'She puffed it all over.' He puffed and huffed, twitched and shook.

'Don't forget Dragon Lady's bats,' said Mad Hatter. 'They were contagious. They spread the fire.' She spread more marmalade on her scone, her seventh by Alix's count.

'Look, I think the fire is a big deal, too. But do we have to discuss it every time we meet?' asked White Rabbit, trying to distract everyone. He pulled his photos out of his vest pocket, convinced that photos of a roof would prove that Caedmon was intact.

Turkey Lurkey said, 'White Rabbit should not have wrecked the building.'

'All he did was tear it down to get the fire out,' said Janus JekyllHyde's lean and sleepy face. 'I'm pleasantly surprised at how good it looks.' He glanced at the photos in White Rabbit's hands, even opening his eyes a bit to see them.

'Whenever I'm pleasantly surprised, you're bitterly disappointed, but when I'm bitterly disappointed, you're pleasantly surprised,' said Janus JekyllHyde's round, alert, frowning face. 'You positively seem to like messes!'

'Janus JekyllHyde possesses many facets,' said Mad Hatter, now eating cherry pie.

'And many faces,' agreed March Hare. She looked first at one face, then the other, trying to remember which was the benevolent one. Her next teapot was shaped like a swan sitting among lotus flowers and leaves, which entwined the body and swirled up above to form a handle. One stalk curved up the swan's neck and opened into the spout. Pink and lavender flowers surrounded the swan's wings. The lid had a handle of lotus stalks, cleverly disguised as decorations.

'I saved the building, I keep telling you!' said White Rabbit. 'We have a perfectly good building, just shorter.' He said this in so positive a manner that everyone looked at him to see if he believed what he was saying.

'Yes, three floors shorter,' said Mad Hatter. 'Can't he see that? And they call me mad. At least I can count.' Alix wondered if Mad Hatter was counting the scones and slices of pie she was eating.

'White Rabbit's practicing the art of administrafiction,' said March Hare. 'Is he convincing Janus?' March Hare changed her place again, moving over to the last clean plate.

'It doesn't matter,' said Mad Hatter. 'Janus is a past grand champion administrafictionist. He'll adjust his story as he needs to.'

Turkey and Janus were still discussing the burning of Caedmon Hall. 'An interesting experiment,' said Turkey Lurkey. 'Some people don't need offices. I do, because my work is so important, as Red Dean said when she gave me two extra labs. Some people only need closets.' He looked at March Hare, knowing that Red Dean had threatened to take her lab away.

Janus JekyllHyde said, 'The new dorms have no closets.'

'No closets?' Turkey Lurkey asked. 'Why not?'

'Red Dean felt that college students wouldn't keep things clean. They would fill the closets with things like dead cats. Another fine mess I don't want to see.'

Alix thought of the students sitting on radiators in the sociolocopathology classroom. Who had decided that they didn't need desks? No desks? No closets? Janus Jekyll-Hyde gave the impression that he decided everything, but he seemed edgy, as if his total control was not so total. Who was he afraid of? Turning towards him, she said, 'I know which classes to avoid, which ones are too crowded.'

'None are too crowded,' said Janus JekyllHyde. 'All are carefully planned. I oversee enrollments very carefully. There are no messes there.' His round face assumed the forward position, forcing the sleepy face towards the back.

'What about the hundreds of students I saw in one class?' asked Alix.

'You are mistaken,' said Janus JekyllHyde. 'I told you, classes are planned carefully. No messes.'

Mad Hatter turned to March Hare. 'How's our party going? Is everyone entertained?' Mad Hatter wore a huge pink Gibson girl hat with an elaborate veil and many ribbons of pale blue, pale green, pale yellow, and peach, matching her long peaches-and-cream dress.

March Hare said, 'One should strive to keep tea conversations as light and frothy as the fare. And it is terribly important to remember to pour milk into the cup before adding the tea. Or is it the other way around?' She turned her hat around, but it looked the same from the back. Flourishing a small teapot shaped like her grandmother's sewing machine, she poured tea into cups shaped like kittens and bunnies and ducklings.

Mad Hatter said, 'We must also strive to avoid accidents. I'll pour the tea in first.' And she did, right into the saucer, which looked like a box turtle.

March Hare said, 'Red Dean blames White Rabbit for the accidents to Mantis and Cuckoo.' She reached for a new teacup, one shaped like a rose.

'What's their problem?' asked Turkey Lurkey, gobbling three watercress sandwiches.

'Preying Praying Mantis is all bent and stiff from hanging over the power line,' said Mad Hatter.

'What's her problem?' asked Turkey Lurkey. Tilting his head at a sharp angle to the left, his contact lenses having slipped again, he ate three cabbage sandwiches.

'That's her problem. She's bent and stiff.' Mad Hatter bent over and became stiff for a moment, causing her hat to topple off, so she found another even larger one of pale orange, with even more ribbons and silk flowers. She tied the ribbons underneath her chin.

'She's always bent and stiff, with fixed claws,' said March Hare, flexing her paws into claws.

'Then why is Red Dean angry?' asked Turkey Lurkey. He drank three cups of tea, no mean feat when you're cockeyed and tilted over.

'One excuse for anger is as good as another,' said Mad Hatter. 'She's angry, White Rabbit's jumpy, that's all that matters.'

'Control,' said Janus, 'is so much easier when everyone is jumpy.' Startled by the sound of a telephone, Janus jumped in his seat.

At that moment, Mad Hatter was in complete control of her hat, her teacup, and her many petticoats.

'Red Dean phoned again,' said March Hare. 'She said we had to hop over to the croquet match right away. She said jump!'

'Is she still on the phone?' asked Mad Hatter, finishing her cherry pie and tea.

'Of course not,' said March Hare. 'You know she hangs up right away. Never a goodbye.'

'Sometimes even before talking,' said Mad Hatter. 'Then it's a relief.'

'She's very, very, very busy, you know,' said Turkey Lurkey, eating a scone. 'She does the work of three men, sometimes working eighteen hours a day.'

'What are her duties?' asked Alix, declining another slice of pie. At last she was full.

'Every little thing,' said Mad Hatter, blowing crumbs off her plate. 'She tends to every little detail. No outside distractions, you know. No family, no friends, no interests outside the institution. So she can spend hours on every detail, working slowly. She corrects every comma, every imagined flaw, every misspelling, every violation of apostrophe rules. And these are faculty documents. I'd hate to see what she'd do to student papers. That's why she works so slowly.'

'Very, very, very slowly, after months of consideration, months. Years. Decades,' said March Hare. 'Deanly decades, we call them.' She looked around the table for a clean plate.

Turkey Lurkey told Alix, 'She has much too muchness of paperwork.'

'Muchness of piles of paper on her desk,' added March Hare. She turned her last plate over so she would have a clean one for the stack of flapjacks she found under the warming cover.

Alix decided to help them clear the table. 'Shall I stack these plates in the kitchen?'

'Oh no, I have a system,' said March Hare, throwing the plates out the window.

'They pile up much too much,' added Mad Hatter, piling many flapjacks on her plate and reaching for the marmalade in a jar shaped like a set of three books with a ceramic kitten playing on top.

'She's a perfectionist. What do you expect?' asked Turkey Lurkey. 'Besides, she has only one assistant.' He poured some more tea into each of his three cups. Aiming for the middle cup, he spilled tea into all of them. His contacts were upside down.

'We're mad,' said Mad Hatter, 'but we finish our work on time. Even without assistants.' She finished her stack of flapjacks right on time to help herself to the new stack coming around the table. She found blueberry jam in a serving jar shaped like a globe and decorated with a kitten sleeping on the Arctic Ocean. The blueberry jam showed through the sides, coloring the oceans blue.

'Oh, she's mad enough,' said March Hare 'Just ask her assistants, who all left. She's plenty mad.'

'They call us mad,' said Mad Hatter, 'but we don't scare anyone away.'

Alix had heard enough talk of madness. There were several types of madness here. Some people, like Janus's round, angry face, were mad for control; some, like Turkey and Dragon Lady, were mad for power; and at least one, Red Dean, was mad with power. But who made the rules? Who decided who was in power? Clearly, Red Dean ran the institution with a stream of E-mail messages. Was she commander in chief? Alix still had to get her new ID and she thought Red Dean's assistant had it. She hoped it wasn't under the piles of paper in Red Dean's office. She felt frustrated at the prospect of replacing her ID, and felt surrounded by confusion both at the mud races and at the party, so she asked March Hare, 'Are your tea parties always so confusing?'

'Only the mad tea parties. Yesterday, we had a real fight. They threw chairs and bottles all over the place. I couldn't find a place to hide, and every time I made a break for the door, somebody knocked me right back inside!'

'Why do they call you mad?' asked Alix, who thought that anyone serving this much food must be sane.

'Some people get to label others,' said Mad Hatter. 'Red Dean is chief labeler. She decides who is mad, who's a troublemaker, who receives a favorable review, who receives a grant, or a paid leave, who's head of each committee, who's on each committee. It's a constant stream of E-mail.'

'Then she makes all the big decisions,' said Alix. 'For example, who's mad, who's bad, who's a good soldier.'

'All the important decisions here,' said March Hare. 'Even names. Mad Hatter's name was Madeleine before Red Dean decided she was uncooperative.'

'I'm going to be late for the croquet match,' said Alix.

'Don't be late,' said Turkey Lurkey. 'She hates that.' His head was now upside down to match his lens.

'What doesn't she hate?' said Alix under her breath.

Alix heard Janus JekyllHyde talking to Turkey Lurkey as they walked to Red Dean's. 'Try to remember—an air of compassion costs nothing, and may get you a lot.' She did not need to see which face was talking. She knew they were both manipulative so it didn't matter.

Mad Hatter serenaded Janus and Turkey as they hurried to Red Dean's croquet match:

The Assistant Professor's First Song

How truly cruel but cruelly true,
To do what we have to do,
We must not what we would.
We must not think too hard and long
Upon the origins of song,
But croak instead
In prose contorted, prose opaque,
About the theory of the Wake:

O leafy bed of adjectives!
A foreigner, as I heard tell,
One who never loved in vain,
Looked into that forest well
And never looked away again.

Chapter Eight

Red Dean's Croquet Match

Alix accompanied March Hare and Mad Hatter to Red Dean's croquet grounds, along a gravel path between lilies, roses, and irises. Reaching the croquet grounds, she could see Red Dean sitting at a table at the far side of the croquet field, talking to those around her. One of her companions seemed to be wearing a purple down overcoat, one a red down overcoat, one a black down overcoat. 'How can anyone be wearing a down coat?' Alix muttered. 'It's cool, but not that cool.' The grass was a relief after the mud course.

Alix couldn't distinguish who was in the overcoats, but she could see Red Dean turn to each person at her table and speak. Alix, having not seen Red Dean since the fire, noticed that she had recovered her balloon shape and bright red color. As she approached, Alix heard Red Dean saying, 'Love. Love. I wrote the book of love. Love . . . freedom . . . freedom . . . freedom's just another word for nothing left to lose. Autonomy . . . fairness. The only things that are important.'

Finally, Alix could see that the coats at the table were just that—coats, without anyone in them, not even chickens or mice or cuckoos. Red Dean must be rehearsing her conversation for later. With no friends, she talks to coats, thought Alix.

Startled by Alix, Red Dean turned. 'It's time you got here. We start soon.'

Alix said, 'I'm eager to play croquet,' hoping she wouldn't have to.

Several people were gathered on the croquet field. Janus JekyllHyde was directing his staff of older faculty—Pigeon, Preying Praying Mantis, Cuckoo, and Turkey Lurkey—who would help him direct the younger members. 'Get the new faculty here. They have to line up. This includes you, Bill.'

Preying Praying Mantis said, 'The new faculty are so pliable.'

'That's why they make such good hoops,' said Turkey Lurkey. 'They bend right over and stay.' Turkey's body was long past the agile shape that made for good hoops, but his head was bent over to see the ground.

'Red Dean said we should count them to make sure they're all here,' said Janus JekyllHyde, counting mallets.

'How many are there?' asked Turkey Lurkey, opening his briefcase and consulting his instructions from Red Dean.

'Go ask Red Dean. She never mentioned the number,' said Janus, handing mallets to the others.

Turkey Lurkey ran over to Red Dean and ran back. 'She doesn't know how many but she says there are lots of them.' He took a mallet from Janus and dropped it on the course.

'Did she give you a list of names?' asked Janus. He was anxious to start the match.

'Not names but numbers. They're all numbers. Red Dean calls them One, Two, Three, Four, Five and so on.'

'And she doesn't know how many?' asked Janus. He waved at the new faculty, signaling them to take their places.

'No, she never counted them. They're just new faculty, without training or shaping or anything,' said Turkey Lurkey. 'They're not important enough for her to remember, I guess.'

'You are mistaken,' said Janus. 'She values them, and she wouldn't call them numbers. She uses names.'

'That's what she said. She said she couldn't remember their names, or which is which, or tell them apart, so she calls each by the number of the order of its hiring. She calls the first one hired One, the second one hired Two, the third Three and so on. It's a perfect system.'

The new faculty were milling about because no one had told them where to go. Pigeon took charge, somewhat. 'All of you come here! Bend over into hoop shapes!'

'I always enjoyed being a hoop,' said Preying Praying Mantis. 'I'll show them what they must do.' And she did, bending over into an angular, upside down *u*.

Cuckoo shouted, 'Students! Form balls! Time for practice!'

'Some students don't make very good balls,' said Pigeon, 'so we'll have to let them roll up as cylinders.' She showed the students how to roll up into tight balls or rigid cylinders, whichever shape was appropriate for their body type. They enjoyed rolling around on the fresh green grass, especially because they were normally not allowed on the field at all.

Alix thought she wouldn't want to be a ball or a cylinder, but she didn't have a student ID, so no one ordered her to roll up. She backed away from Pigeon and Cuckoo, hoping they wouldn't ask. She hid among some lilac bushes.

Janus JekyllHyde recited the rules. 'Students! If you hit your head and are unconscious, even momentarily, you must take yourself out of the match.' His little mustache waved up and down like a flag against his round frown.

'That doesn't make sense,' said Alix. 'How can anyone take himself out if he's unconscious?'

'You are mistaken,' said Janus JekyllHyde. 'This is the most efficient method of maintaining order, just as effective as our registration methods.' He began putting signs near the hoops. His lean Stan Laurel face was fast asleep.

'How can you say that?' asked Alix. 'Some classes have hundreds of students, too many for the classroom, and some have only three. Is that effective registration?' She thought of Windy Hole and Mazin Grates.

'You are mistaken,' said Janus. 'The classes are small so the students feel valued. You heard Red Dean at the assembly. This is very important. The students must feel valued.' He knocked a student ball, sort of kicking her, out of his way. His sleepy face awoke at the thump of the student body.

'How can they feel valued when they have to roll through hoops?' Alix stared at the students practicing to be misshapen balls, rolling about and bumping into hoops.

'How else do you expect them to fulfill their requirements?' Janus looked in every direction, each face scanning about so he could see everywhere at once. He put the rest of the signs near hoops, mashing down the tulip and daffodil leaves to level the field.

'What about the huge classes I saw in Windy Hole? Are you going to do something about them?' Alix watched two students bump into each other, then crash into a third ball.

Janus said, 'The reason nothing has been done is because no one has made any effort to do anything about it.' Sometimes the truth slipped out of Janus's second face.

'I think it's irresponsible,' said Alix, who saw that Janus certainly made an effort to do something about faculty. Why wouldn't he do something about overcrowded classes? A lopsided student ball rolled into a hoop and knocked it over. Something about this exercise reminded Alix of movies of boot camp, Marine boot camp. The iris bed seemed out of place. Barbed wire would have fit the mood of the match.

'There you go, thinking again,' said Janus. 'You'll make mistakes if you do. You're already mistaken.' Satisfied the signs were well placed and the students doing about as well as one could expect from beginners, Janus cried out in a loud voice, 'Let the match begin!'

And it did. Pigeon, Turkey Lurkey, and Preying Praying Mantis began knocking students through hoops. Turkey was pleased. 'See, the students are already expanding their perspectives as they learn the process.' They were, but some were crying, as loud as Dragon Lady's baby. Others were shouting encouragement at their friends. Alix also heard curses.

'The thing is,' said Pigeon, 'they're also going through orientation sessions.'

One student rolled near Alix. 'This one has a head that looks like a watermelon with a fur coat on,' said Alix. 'What's wrong? Her head is all swollen! And lopsided!'

'A few knocks, a few crashes into other balls,' said Pigeon. 'She's meeting other students. She's becoming part of our community.'

Cuckoo addressed her ball: 'Stay! Thou art so fair!' Then she hit it hard. 'That's the greatest shot I ever saw in my life. Of course, the wind was with me, and I'm young.'

Preying Praying Mantis said, 'If you'd hit it perfectly, it would have been even better.' She whacked her ball hard, right into a sand trap. 'I'm playing better and better,' said Preying Praying Mantis. 'But I think Janus resents a good woman player. He's changing the rules.' Body contorted to a corkscrew, she mashed her ball as hard as she could.

'That's so true,' said Cuckoo. 'If a woman has anything on the ball, men feel threatened.' Looking around the

croquet grounds, she said, 'Someone has done some significant gardening here.' Then she whacked the ball out of
the field and into the parking lot. 'That'll teach them to
bring their Volvos.'

Pigeon and Turkey were watching Cuckoo. Pigeon said,
'I think I'm going to like what I think I'm going to get to
know about Cuckoo.' Then she knocked her ball off the
field, too.

'How do you think she's doing so far?' asked Turkey.
He swung his mallet but missed the ball, for now his bifo-
cal contact lenses were sideways, so that the up-close lens
flanked his beak. This time he was really cross-eyed.

'She doesn't know how to be herself because she does-
n't know who she is,' said Pigeon, kicking her ball back
onto the croquet grounds.

Turkey thought of some faculty he had known for
years. 'Is that a disadvantage?' He swung again, missed
again.

'Only if she wants to rise to the top. Compliant faculty
could assume twenty or even ten years ago that they had
a greased skid to the top,' said Janus. 'Look at your own
success.'

'What! No way!' said Turkey. 'I made it, made tenure
and professor, on my own. I gave up every other activity
to concentrate on writing. I shut out my family, colleagues,
and students and spent every evening, every weekend,
every summer in my office or lab.' He whacked a student
ball vigorously into a hoop labeled Inquiry into Realism.

'You are mistaken,' said Janus. 'We decided long ago
to push you to the top—you were the most compliant one
of your cohort.' He knocked his student ball through the
next hoop, Creative Exposure, the CE requirement.

'But I've published. I'm famous in my field. I earned
tenure,' said Turkey. He hit his ball, trying to catch Janus
and fulfill the requirement for his student.

'You are mistaken,' said Janus. 'Tenure is granted by
decree. You saw Lizard Bill's modifications.' Janus tapped

his ball into Turkey's student, then sent Turkey's student rocketing off the course into a thick clump of spirea, where it got caught.

'I wasn't altered like that. Bill changed color and shape and skin.' Turkey kicked his ball back onto the field.

'We didn't have to force you. You changed shape on command.' Janus shoved his ball towards the next hoop, Mystography.

Because some students didn't fit through hoops, the croquet match was becoming chaotic, so Red Dean landed to supervise the foursome of Duck, Goose, Slug, and Drone.

'Why don't those balls fit?' she shouted. 'Trim their heads! Cut off any heads that don't fit through the hoops. Trim their feet. Where's Dragon Lady? She should be here with her team.'

Alix said to Drone, 'I thought Dragon Lady was her ally.'

'Red Dean has no allies. Just subordinates.' Drone carefully patted his student into a tight ball. His student was quite tall, so his legs tended to stick out.

'And subordinatesses,' added Slug. He rolled his student through TNT, or The Numbing Theory.

'What about friends?' asked Alix. She was thinking of Red Dean talking to her coats.

'Friends?' said Drone. 'She has rebuttals but no friends.' He nudged his student through EASY—Elementary Analysis of Statistical Years.

'I thought I heard her conversing,' said Alix, 'but she was rehearsing her conversation by talking to overcoats.'

'There you have it,' said Drone. 'She rehearses all conversations. But when she converses, she seems to prefer objects that don't talk back. Then she doesn't have to deal with their responses. She likes it better, I'm sure.' He whispered to his student, 'Well done! You've fulfilled the Mathemessics requirement.'

Red Dean bobbed up to them and said, 'Send Dragon Lady over. Some of the faculty need help in getting flat enough to bend over.' She pushed a few hoops into shape and hissed, 'Stay, Four! Maintain your posture, Three! Quit flopping, Five!'

Alix edged away and joined Duck and Goose as they softly pushed their balls.

'They can never begin to pay me enough for all I do around here,' said Duck.

'The pay is unfair,' agreed Goose. 'How many June bugs did you get last year?'

'Very few. Who decides how many we get?' Duck eased a student ball around a hoop and checked off the student's form to show she had completed CA, the Cultured Arts requirement.

'Red Dean,' said Goose. 'Think she'd let anyone else?' Since Goose's student was too big to easily fit, Goose flattened the hoop for him to roll over it and called it 'swooping.'

Slug said, 'She insisted we should be happy with what we get because we have tenure.' He pretended to swing his mallet at his student so Red Dean could see him at play.

'She's happy with what she gets,' said Duck. 'She's much bigger than I am.' Duck pushed his student through SIT, Speaking in Tongues, and waddled toward Cultured Arts.

'Thank heaven tenure review is only once, if you make it,' said Goose. 'Now I don't have to bend over hooply, as she calls it. But I'm constantly evaluated, and I'm constantly on tenure review for others.' He looked at the poor faculty hoops, all stained and strained.

'Constant evaluations. Constant reviews. Endless committees,' said Drone, heading for the next requirement, CY —Computing You—a hoop deep in shadows under elm trees.

'When I teach, it's a relief,' said Goose. 'A relief from evaluations, committees, and constant reviews.'

'I enjoy teaching,' said Slug. 'The class is mine to control, and the students are cooperative.' His student rolled herself through the next hoop, AA, Advanced Analysis.

'I became a teacher because I like the students and the subject,' said Duck. 'I thought that being a professor I'd have real control over my life. I didn't count on Red Dean.'

'Why does she talk of autonomy?' asked Alix, watching the students, most of whom were grass-stained all over. It was hard to tell one from another.

'Why does she talk of lots of things she doesn't really believe in?' said Duck. She's full of hot air, that's why.' His student rolled through the final hoop and earned her COC—Certificate of Completion.

'The constant evaluations are the worst,' said Goose. 'I thought once I had tenure, I could relax and teach and feel safe, but the pressure got worse.' He urged his student through FLAM, Foreign, Lateral, Analytical Math, a pooped hoop if there ever was one—it drooped in the middle and on both sides.

Slug nodded. 'When I commented on the pressure, she said, "Get out if you don't like it," but this is my career.' He pushed his student quickly after Goose's through FLAM, while the hoop was still open.

Duck sighed. 'They say we're to blame for our own unhappiness,' and aimed his student towards SSS—Self, Selfism, and Society—and gave her a gentle push. 'This is extra credit,' he whispered.

'Red Dean says we're too passive, that we cause our own problems,' said Goose. 'Sometimes I wish she'd simply remove me, as she has so many others.' His student caught up to Duck's at the SSS hoop and followed her through just before the hoop collapsed.

Duck said, 'She told me, "If your work makes you miserable, you must be doing it wrong," but I reject that.'

The foursome saw that they had completed the requirements for their students, so they left quickly, before Red
Dean or Janus thought of more hoops for them to fulfill.

Mad Hatter and March Hare were riding their teacart,
motorized and still running, from hoop to hoop, but it
looked battered and bruised. Their teapots and scones
were clattering and bouncing around with them. March
Hare had packed her simplest teapots, the pineapple, the
coconut, the mango, and the artichoke-shaped teapots.
They rolled around inside the cart whenever the students
dropped them.

Mad Hatter's competition outfit was a black chiffon
flared skirt, a hand-crocheted jacket of red silk flowers
stitched together in a loose, lacy weave, and her biggest
straw hat, a red flat-brimmed sombrero with black roses
and orchids. She also wore sling-back three-inch heels,
because she had no plans whatsoever to walk through the
course. She would ride.

Dragon Lady landed near Mad Hatter and March Hare
to ask them about the field. 'What are all those unsightly
lumps all over the croquet grounds?'

'Scatterbrains,' said Mad Hatter. 'Brains are scattered
all over. Red Dean made us trim students.' She hoped this
would gross out Dragon Lady enough to make her fly
away.

'There's been much bashing about of brains,' said
March Hare, helping herself to tea. Her croquet-match
outfit was a purple rayon leisure suit with bright folk designs of fish and flowers embroidered along the front of
the jacket. She wore a black flat-brimmed Spanish hat.

'I always said you two were mad,' said Dragon Lady.
'Why is your croquet cart so funny-looking? Were you two
in a wreck?' She kicked a tire, rattling the tea set.

'We've never had a wreck,' answered March Hare, 'at
least not to our knowledge.' She poured tea for Mad Hatter
and offered cucumber sandwiches around.

'Our croquet cart was mangled in a car wash,' added Mad Hatter, offering Dragon Lady some carrot cake. Their student balls were hiding in the tea cart, enjoying scones and carrot cake while Mad Hatter and March Hare collected their requirements.

'Why do I waste my time here?' asked Dragon Lady. 'I could be in Perth. I do so miss the theatre in Toledo and Sydney.' She handed Mad Hatter the empty plate.

'What odd names. Perth. Sydney,' said March Hare, closing the door of the teacart so Dragon Lady wouldn't see the students inside.

'They're glorious names! Sydney. Syyyyydney,' said Dragon Lady. 'Your name, by the way, means "hardware," so you wouldn't know about glorious names.'

'Hardware?' said March Hare. 'Hare means "swift." Your name, by the way, means "snake." Dragon means "snake." '

'Snakes don't fly, so there,' said Dragon Lady and flew off.

'And they call us mad,' said Mad Hatter. The two of them carefully eased their students out of hiding, then through the last hoop, AAA, Ancient Alternative Abstractions, thus obtaining all of the Perspectives. As usual, March Hare and Mad Hatter's students were among the first to finish, so they retired to a snack stand for refreshments and Mad Hatter's song:

Sitting in an Office, or The Old Frog's Lament

Little fish, I miss you so, I miss your mazy tail,
Which waved so prettily about when you fetched the evening mail.

How I miss those luffly days when at the screen you sat,
Computing all those messages about the dean's red hat
She sported at commencement when the band began to play
And both of you marched bravely in to awe us at croquet.
The hoops! The hoops! O how we yearned to conquer them for her,

To squeeze ourselves so rightly tight and roll obscenely far.
Alas, those days when we were young professors in our prime
Have fled to fields where Red Deans Dance to two-four time.
Your mazy fins, your mazy fins! How bravely waved they then
When we were young professors and she the Great Red Dean.

Chapter Nine

Courses and Classes,
Coming and Going

R ed Dean continued to supervise the croquet match,
since it had not been going as smoothly as she
liked. Some balls had lost their roundness, some had
fallen into gopher holes, and some hoops had collapsed,
perhaps from exhaustion, but that was no excuse in her
opinion. All of the balls and most of the hoops were
stained green, and the balls had an additional layer of
black from the dirt they had picked up in the flower beds.

Red Dean inhaled, and inhaled, and became larger than
ever, and her face as red as her dress. 'No wonder she's
named Red,' said Alix. 'Big Red Dean.' Red Dean now
filled out all the folds of her tent dress and it stood out
like a canopy.

Red Dean hollered at the students, 'Tuck in those
hands! Get your feet in!' as some of the students unrolled.

Alix saw a couple of them crawl off into some lilac bushes and hide. Then she saw one student suddenly unroll herself, stand up, and stretch. Next thing, the student was dashing away very fast, heading for the dorm. 'I've had a wonderful time. Now I have to go,' she shouted as she ran away.

Red Dean called Turkey Lurkey and Caterpillar to help. 'Trim those hands! Trim those feet! Cut off any head or hand or foot that won't fit through the hoops! Everyone has to fit through the hoops.' Alix wondered what the students were learning here. Autonomy? Fairness? Freedom?

'Why do we have to fit?' asked a student with long legs and arms. 'I'll never squeeze through those hoops. I'm bigger than they are.'

'You must go through each hoop,' said Turkey Lurkey. 'How else do you expect to fulfill your requirements?' He pounded some loose feet into a proper round student ball.

'You've already been told about the Process Requirements,' said Caterpillar, puffing on his pipe. 'You must be processed and we're here to make sure you process the right way. It wouldn't do for you to knock over a hoop or go through one backwards. So we monitor your progress.'

'When do we get to choose our classes?' asked a student named Kim.

Caterpillar puffed on his pipe and blew smoke rings that swirled around his body and inside his shirt, creating a puffy, stuffed look.

'What is the optimum college education?' asked Caterpillar. 'My pipe dream is that one day we will have a cooperative effort between parents, students, school, and professors. These are the people that care and have no profit to gain from it. Education is more than do you or do you not have a course. That's the least part of it.' Smoke rings circled his head.

'Did you understand that?' Kim asked Chad, the tall student. Her voice, usually loud, was almost a whisper and they began retreating into the trees.

'I don't think even Caterpillar understood himself,' answered Chad, looking at Caterpillar's smoking shirt. 'His speech was so stuffy—but I guess that's what I would expect from a stuffed shirt.' Chad found a garden shed they could hide in.

'What about all those speeches about active learning?' asked Kim. 'When do we get active?' She jogged and danced and jumped over some student balls and cylinders on her way to the shed.

'Perhaps this is active learning,' said Alix, 'getting knocked, pushed, kicked through the requirements, watching more and more students rolling about the croquet grounds.' But she winced as she saw students banging into each other. If this was active learning, why was it so chaotic, and what exactly were these students supposed to be learning? How to take hard knocks? How to hide and ride through the requirements? How to circumvent Red Dean's orders?

White Rabbit said, 'All of these students are gaining perspectives, actively learning where the hoops are and what each represents. They're actively learning to fulfill requirements.' Alix wanted to ask what was the educational value in collecting absurd requirements, but she knew that White Rabbit wouldn't understand her objections. He thought everything was nicely ordered and coherent.

'I should meet with my advisor again,' said Alix. 'The first meeting was not at all helpful. I still don't know what classes to take.' I know some to avoid, she thought.

'Who is your advisor?' asked White Rabbit, shoving his student through Inquiry into Racism. Thorny shrub roses and a carpet of poison ivy surrounded this hoop.

'Caterpillar,' said Alix. 'He wasn't enlightening.'

'There's something positive about light,' said White Rabbit. 'Who was it who said, "Let there be light"?'

'Maybe I'll find my own classes,' said Alix, edging away. White Rabbit seemed to be getting more mad each time she met him.

Holding a lemon in each hand, Preying Praying Mantis began directing the faculty hoops. 'Hold your hoops high, everyone. Keep yourselves rigid!'

'Easy for her to say,' said Pigeon. 'She's permanently rigid.'

Preying Praying Mantis bent her body into an angular hoop. 'Look, everybody, do it like this.' Her expression was as sour as the lemons she was eating.

'Bending and making a hoop comes easily to Preying Mantis's body,' said Alix to Pigeon. 'But why is she so adamant about the proper form for everyone else?'

'She's adamant about everything,' said Pigeon. 'Has she checked your prayer yet?' Pigeon tried cooing to her student ball as they approached Physical Abstractions. The ball was shivering.

'My prayer?'

Henny Penny, running to meet them, said, 'She checks everyone's prayer, especially those of new faculty members. She's Praying Mantis, after all.' Using her trusty ladder as a mallet, she tapped her student ball through HP, Hysterical Perspectives. The hoop was freaking out in fear of Red Dean.

'How does she check prayers?' asked Alix. 'Do people have to give copies to her?'

Henny Penny said, 'She's compulsive about purity. She says she believes in personal choice, but the choice must match hers. She's going to match us to death!' Henny urged her student to roll through IA, Interpretation of Analysis, a pretzel-shaped hoop even skinnier than Preying Praying Mantis.

'Can she enforce her choices?' asked Alix.

'No, but here comes someone who can!' shouted Pigeon, running for the HF, the Healthy Fitness hoop. Alix noticed once again how eager Pigeon was to please Red Dean, but also avoid her.

Red Dean said, 'Get over here! Everyone must play. We're a community.'

'Another free-choice person,' commented Alix. 'Well, I hate to run, but I've got to find my advisor and choose courses.' Actually, she had begun to think she might choose her own courses. Caterpillar had not been at all helpful when she had tried to talk with him. He had general theories but no specific answers. She saw three more students unroll and run away. They were probably exercising their autonomy.

Later that afternoon Alix walked past the remains of Caedmon Hall and saw the former residents perching in nearby trees. Magpie was weaving a nest. Cuckoo was creeping closer and closer to her, obviously trying to size it up for future use, being a nest-stealer. Duck, Goose, and Crab had moved to the pond and built homes on the muskrat mounds. Henny Penny was crying, 'They want us to freeze out here! But we'll probably fall out of the trees first and break our necks!'

'I'm looking for Caterpillar,' Alix told Janus Jekyll-Hyde. 'I tried to talk to him at the croquet match but he disappeared into blue smoke.'

'Are you sure he's a caterpillar?' asked Janus, frowning, 'Some people are unreliable.'

'I'm not at all sure,' said Alix, 'of that, or anything else. I'm not sure he's a caterpillar or slug or worm, but I hate to ask. He takes offense easily, and besides, I usually can't understand his answers.' She'd begun to think that his brain was surrounded by blue smoke, and inefficient.

'There is nothing in nature as magical as the moment when a moth turns into a butterfly,' said the lean-face Janus, who obviously had slept through his Insectology for Beginners hoop. Janus pointed to a band of red tape running from tree to tree and off towards a building and said, 'Follow it faithfully.'

Alix thought Janus was beginning to sound as confusing as Caterpillar, but she didn't like to say so, so she followed the red tape to Boiling Point, the administration building. She wanted to read the various course descriptions on the bulletin boards.

The first one read, Researchification: four credits; six class hours of lecture; two labs, four hours each.

'Too much time,' said Alix as she followed the red tape dividers to the next section.

Sci-Fi Research, then Hydroglyphics: Water Writing Above and Below, then Introductory Bridgics. Alix followed the red tape to the next board. There she found Introductory Geolocation Department: Salivary Deposits, Excrementory Deposits.

She saw some other students beyond the red tape dividers and asked one of them about the courses. 'Are these courses still open?'

The student, whose name was Paul, said, 'Of course they're open. Who would want them?'

'Can you recommend any classes?' asked Alix.

'I like the Dangerous Thinking Department,' said Paul. He pointed to Invertrics, Negative Capabilities, Premenitionology, Integretity, and Phallicisms.

Alix saw that these classes were closed, so she read the description of Phenomenology and the Meaning of Realism. The description began, 'The logical investigation extends this notion of psychologically constituted, but not psychologistically analyzable, objectivity to all the entities of reason which occur in logical theory: to the infinitely various senses or meanings, misguidedly called "concepts," which occur in thought. . . ' Seeing that she was not even one-third through the sentence, she gave up, on the sentence and on the course.

She felt startled at the next title, Shrew Studies. 'How can anyone offer this course nowadays?'

Paul said, 'It's not what you're thinking. It's a biology course. It's real shrews. They appropriated the title after Humane Etudes dropped it.'

Alix then saw a board titled Human Metrics and read the listings. Sociometrics, Psychometrics, and Anthrometrics. 'These seem too mathematical,' she decided. 'Where's the bulletin board for Humane Etudes?'

'Here's the list,' said Paul. 'Formal Expansion, Introduction to Interpretation, Advanced Exposure, Dillentology.'

'What about this course, Intoleratude?'

'Stay away!' He looked so horrified that Alix didn't bother to ask why.

By now she felt frustrated. 'How do you pick courses?'

'I sometimes pick the professor,' said Paul, 'and I pick some to avoid.'

'Can you recommend some?'

'I avoid Professor Piper. He's popular and has quite a following of devoted students, but he has two tests for picking his female assistants: First, can you see your feet without bending over? If a woman cannot, she's hired. And second, when you approach a wall with your hands at your sides, is your nose the first part of your body that touches?'

'He's only interested in one thing!' cried Alix.

'Yes, well, two,' said Paul. 'Meet me in the Study Lounge tonight and I'll help you choose. I don't want to be overheard giving you tips.'

Alix thought Paul might be overreacting, but she didn't say anything. If he didn't want to be overheard, he must know best.

As Paul left, Alix heard Ostrich and Parrot talking as they walked out of Ostrich's office. Ostrich said, 'I had hoped Prince Charles would marry Linda Ronstadt, but don't ask me why.' His huge wings made a shrugging gesture.

Parrot said, 'And people laughed at you for that. He'd be better off. He's just now started Phase II of his maturation process.' He shrugged his own long blue wings. Ostrich meant well, but was out of the loop.

Ostrich said, 'If it's all right with you, I thought today we'd start our long-range planning.'

'We're in this together,' replied Parrot. He'd heard other proposals for long-range planning before—the last one planned a rifle range. 'Have you heard about Piper's fact-finding trip to the East Coast? He found rare spices and fine silks.'

'Wasn't he supposed to find facts to help The Course? It needs facts to survive.'

'What can you expect? He's Piper.' Parrot tried to exit the door and the conversation.

Ostrich said, 'He's a man who knows what he wants but he's a man that nobody wants.' He followed Parrot into the hall.

'Except some of his groupies,' said Parrot, stepping towards the outside door.

'Chiefly his male groupies,' said Ostrich, 'who admire his ability to get paid for these fact-finding trips. I guess it's a guy thing. They want to know his secret of getting free trips.' Ostrich enjoyed a free trip now and then himself, since his wings were too tiny for flying.

Parrot took a few more steps toward the door. 'He's a little frog in a big pond, but we need little frogs.' He touched the doorknob and hoped Ostrich would get the signal that he was leaving.

'I'll rescue him if he gets out of his depth,' said Ostrich, who actually believed he could.

'Don't you find him oddly stuffy for someone of limited ability?' Parrot knew Ostrich couldn't rescue Piper— he was too far outside the loop.

'Stuffy is a defense mechanism, according to the Psychos,' said Ostrich.

'They would know,' agreed Parrot. 'They're all stuffed. Well, another ninety minutes of my life down the drain. Why did we have this meeting anyway?'

'If you don't know why I called you in here, and I don't know why I called you in here, I don't suppose anybody in the world knows why I called you in here,' Ostrich said, looking back at his office. He held his ring of keys in one hand and the list of faculty members' phone numbers, fax numbers, and E-mail addresses in the other. He was in contact with everyone.

'Make that ninety-five minutes,' said Parrot and ran out while Ostrich was distracted with his lists.

Overhearing the conversation between Ostrich and Parrot, Alix was sure that neither of them was in charge of the institution. For one thing, they were too mild. She hurried out of the building but unfortunately encountered Red Dean and Dragon Lady near the entrance. The match over, many of the student balls followed the trail of red tape into Boiling Point to get their requirements validated. They were carrying tokens proving they had finished their orientation sessions and expanded their perspectives. But the match was not over for certain hoops. Some of the younger faculty had collapsed around the student balls.

'Dismiss them! Dismiss them immediately!' Red Dean shouted. Her body quivered in anger, sending wobbly waves through her dress, a long, fuschia-flowered tent dress. Her necklaces included a Star of David pendant, a Byzantine cross, a silver prayer wheel Zen pendant, and an Irish cross with Celtic designs. They jangled as she shouted. Today she celebrated multi-religions.

'Who?' asked Dragon Lady, quivering in synch, though more in apprehension than anger. She seemed thinner and thinner every time Alix saw her. Her wings wrapped twice around her body now. Her thin black hair was now short and frosted.

'Dismiss all the hoops who didn't maintain posture during the match!' Red Dean gasped. 'I can't have people flopping about as they want to.' She flapped her arms and rattled her gold coin bracelets. Her Roman coins, Greek coins, Egyptian, and Spanish coins jangled loudly.

'They weren't flopping about. They were standing up to breathe.' Dragon Lady backed away, afraid an explosion was coming.

'Who gave them permission to breathe? Dismiss them!' Red Dean gasped three times, expanding her size significantly.

'What about Six? She fainted. She didn't disobey.' Dragon Lady had tried to revive Six.

'Dismissssssssss!' hissed Red Dean, then gasped to restore her air supply.

'And Two? The students love him!' said Dragon Lady.

'Love! Love? Love means never having to say you're sorry.'

'Who do you want to keep?' asked Dragon Lady.

Red Dean paused for a moment. 'Searches are so expensive. Let's keep four of them, ummmm One, Three, Five, Seven—how's that?' Red Dean floated away, like a balloon, which, after all, she was.

'Well, not as bad as last year,' said Dragon Lady. 'Maybe losing her air and Caedmon Hall changed her.'

Alix approached Dragon Lady. 'Do you think she's becoming more . . . uh . . .?' Alix couldn't think of a good word. 'Humane' didn't fit; neither did 'nice.'

'Nothing ever really changes with her,' said Dragon Lady, 'no matter what shape she's in because it's all hot air inside. All form, no content. She had to adjust her dismissals because of unexpected expenses. She simply couldn't dismiss as many as usual because searches are so expensive, but she still thinks the same way. Nobody's able to measure up. Nobody is perfect enough for a perfectionist.'

Alix felt sorry for Dragon Lady, who tried so hard to please Red Dean, who tried so hard to be a team player, who had to guess what the requirements were, who had to guess who else was in favor at the moment. Alix thought of how much Dragon Lady had changed in the last few hours. She was so skinny now. Alix herself had changed, and not only her clothes. Her hair was tangled; her glasses were gone. 'I seem to be a different person altogether,' she said quietly. 'I don't think I'm at all the person I was yesterday.' She wanted to go back to Caedmon Hall to find her backpack so she could get her ID, backpack, and Puppy, and maybe feel more like herself.

Chapter Ten

Lobster Quadrille

Goose found Alix outside Boiling Point and invited her to the PIC, the Picnic for the Institutional Community, in the central mall among the flowers and trees. It had been decorated with streamers and banners, one reading Communication Builds Community. Alix saw several pavilions in several different colors. The nearest one was pale yellow to indicate the pale foods: rice cakes, flapjacks, lefse, glorified rice, and casseroles of noodles, corn, and cream of mushroom soup with Tater Tots on top. 'We find it more convenient for everyone when the food is color-coded,' said Ostrich.

Goose stepped over to the brown canopy, where he got bratwurst, brownies, and root beer. 'See? A complete meal!' said Ostrich, glowing with happiness. 'And everything is brown!'

Suddenly, Red Dean, Dragon Lady, and White Rabbit rushed past Alix and Ostrich, who said, 'Now that the croquet match is over, Red Dean must begin the Lobster Quadrille.'

'What's the Lobster Quadrille?' asked Alix, shaking her head to indicate her refusal of baked beans and bratwurst.

'We decide who goes, who stays; it's a dance,' answered Ostrich, helping himself to brownies and coffee. To maintain the color scheme, the tables were decorated with brown (as in dead) flower heads.

'For students?' Alix hoped she wouldn't have to join. She decided against a brownie.

'For staff. Sometimes faculty participate,' said Ostrich. 'We have to move out old blood, move in new.' Ostrich moved out from under the canopy, and Duck joined Goose and Alix.

'How about administrators?' asked Alix. She followed Ostrich back to the yellow tent, where he got some glorified rice and a cream soda.

Duck was shocked. 'Oh, no! Not administrators. They stay until they're too tired to go on, or too slow to understand, or till they drop, and often much beyond. It's positively inspiring!'

'Who decides when they're too tired?'

'They do, of course. Sometimes they test each other, but usually they all decide about themselves. They prefer it that way,' said Ostrich.

'Aren't they evaluated? I know that faculty are often evaluated,' said Alix.

'Yes, faculty have to survive many evaluations from students, peers, superiors, but the reviews for administrators are just formalities,' said Goose as they rejoined him in the yellow tent. 'No matter what the results are, each is reappointed by a superior, so the administrators go on and on until they are too tired to hang on.' Goose ate some creamed corn and scalloped potatoes. 'They don't know, or don't follow, the old saying, "When you're dead, lie down," so they go on and on.'

'What about the faculty review committees?' asked Alix. 'Don't they periodically evaluate administrators?' She began walking towards a red, green, and white canopy, hoping it indicated Italian food. It was surrounded by bright red lilies, white phlox, and green hydrangea flowers. Alix thought she could smell pizza, bread, and pasta mingling with the smell of the phlox.

'We let faculty think they have a say,' answered Ostrich, coming with his banana from the yellow pavilion.

'Students are on all review committees, aren't they?' asked Alix, looking at spinach lasagna. It looked marvelous! Just marvelous!

'Certainly. It makes them equal in power to faculty, Red Dean says,' said Goose, stepping around the hydrangea to get some ravioli.

Alix heard Red Dean calling for Janus JekyllHyde and Turkey Lurkey. 'Get over here! We have to evaluate staff today!' By now Alix, Ostrich, and Goose were across the mall from her.

'What will she do today?' asked Alix, helping herself to a taco. She remembered that Mexico's colors were also green, red, and white, like Italy's. The white wheat taco had tomatoes inside and guacamole on the top.

'Well, she usually has them play musical chairs,' said Goose. 'Then she removes a chair, and someone has to go.' Goose stepped toward a tub of sodas, strawberry, lime, and cream.

'Doesn't she select the person?' Alix was curious to see how this was done.

'Not officially. She says it's more fair to let staff fight over the remaining chairs, but she gets someone to trip the person she wants removed. When he doesn't get to a chair, he's out. She can then explain that there simply isn't room, that the position has vanished.' Goose's foot vanished into the tub as he stepped into it by mistake.

'Does she remove staff or administrators this way?'

'Staff, always. Administrators stick together. She wouldn't remove one of her own. It would look bad,' said Goose. 'Besides, this way, she can deny any favoritism. The chair is gone, and that person is out of a position.' Goose and Alix crept closer to Red Dean to hear whom she planned to dismiss.

Red Dean told Janus JekyllHyde, 'We decided that Boar is out of touch and that you are to tell him.' Janus's lean and sleepy face instantly swung towards the back, and even his control face blanched and quivered.

Goose whispered to Alix, 'Red Dean is afraid of Boar. She's scared he'll puncture her with his tusks. Boar is an unusual success story. From institutional goon to vice president: all done with tusks.'

Because Boar's office was a gazebo with many holes in the walls, they could see him sitting on a huge, ornate gold throne on a raised dais, surrounded by dozens of filing cabinets.

'He has records of every student in the history of the institution. He keeps them forever,' said Dodo. 'He says you never know when you might have to check on a person.'

Goose added, 'His records probably cover more than students. The rumors are that he has files on everyone who ever worked here. He spread the rumors, I'm sure.' Goose spread his large wings. 'Only Red Dean has more records. She logs each E-mail message, keeps hard copies of all her directives and all the responses. E-mail was supposed to cut down paper records, but it has taken up three floors of Boiling Point.'

Alix said, 'He must have a lot of staff. There are dozens of filing cabinets and lots of computer storage discs in there.'

'Dozens of staff,' agreed Dodo, 'he once had dozens, but he chased them into corners and onto the roof.'

'Why?' asked Alix, trying to picture staff members on the roof of the gazebo. It looked shaky with all the holes in the walls. And the gazebo was hardly large enough for Boar's throne and all the filing cabinets.

'So they'll obey better,' said Goose. 'He always says a scared staff listens better.'

Alix watched Boar sitting on his throne. Because of all the holes in the outer walls, she could hear him saying, 'This is where I do some of my best work.'

'His job is safe then,' said Alix, 'if Red Dean and Dragon Lady are scared of him. Normally they enjoy terrorizing subordinates, but Boar has them terrorized. Where are his subordinates?'

'See the holes in the walls?' asked Goose. 'Subordinates running away from him ran right through the walls, making the holes. Since he moved to the gazebo, all the staff ran away.' The gazebo area looked like a war zone— craters, chunks of brick, piles of concrete left over from construction, gravel, roof shingles, and half-empty pails of roofing tar. No plants marred its industrial decor.

'When he was still in Boiling Point he had staff,' said Duck, walking by towards his new office. 'They couldn't break through the walls.' Duck left to claim a new office near Caedmon.

Boar dictated into his recorder, 'I'm planning to have myself cloned. This place needs more like me.'

'Is Boar the worst bully here?' asked Alix, walking through the trees at the edge of the campus. The cottonwoods were releasing fluffy seeds, and it looked like a summer snowstorm. Alix loved the rustle of the cottonwoods, the sound reminding her of a brook.

'Depends,' said Goose. 'Have you met Gila Monster?'

'No,' said Alix. 'Where is he?'

'She. See this big square building?' Goose pointed to a square building with many windows, surrounded by many trees. 'She looks harmless. She says she represents a new softer image of womankind, and she has a big smile like all gila monsters, but she's poisonous. She's already killed four staff members in the two years she's been here and she has several more bites planned.' Goose began eating the popcorn he'd carried from the yellow pavilion.

'Bites! She bites?' Alix made a mental note of someone else to avoid. Boar, Dragon Lady, Red Dean, Janus Jekyll-Hyde, Turkey Lurkey, Preying Praying Mantis, even her advisor Caterpillar. The list was growing.

'That's how gila monsters kill,' said Goose. 'She's determined to replace the whole staff within five years.' Goose finished eating his popcorn and, seeing Red Dean and Dragon Lady and White Rabbit approach, left for his office with quite a rapid step for a goose. Maybe he had his own list of people to avoid.

Alix followed Red Dean, Dragon Lady, and White Rabbit to the ruins of Caedmon Hall, still stinking from the fire. Cuckoo, Preying Praying Mantis, Pigeon, Duck, and Caterpillar were in trees nearby. It looked even worse than White Rabbit's photo, black, smoky, and broken.

Cuckoo watched Red Dean approaching. 'Let's hope she doesn't look up and see us,' she said, and she shrunk herself behind some leaves, quit chirping, and covered her pink and orange head.

'She's too tired to bounce up here,' said Duck. 'Why can't she see how tired she is and retire?' Duck was living at the pond, but his office was still officially at Caedmon, so he had a tree branch to himself where he kept his desk and files. As soon as he saw Alix, he called out, 'Alix, we found your backpack—wet but still containing most of your belongings. I hung your stuffed animal in the sun to dry.'

'Puppy! You found Puppy!' cried Alix. She saw Puppy pinned to a branch and retrieved him, then she looked into her backpack only to find that her wallet was there but all of her papers, even her identification card from the institution, had been washed clean of writing. She felt blank, her identity washed off.

Goose told her, 'Janus is in charge of registration, but Red Dean's office issues ID cards. You'll have to go there for a new card. You'll need some other form of identification to obtain a new card. Here comes Red Dean now—you can ask her what to do.'

When Alix looked at Red Dean, then at the faculty, she decided to wait until later. Every one of the inhabitants of the trees was trying to avoid her, and Alix did not want to draw her attention to them. Goose and Duck had become very quiet as everyone watched Red Dean approaching.

'As soon as she's gone, I'm going to the back yard to write love letters in the sand,' said Cuckoo, waving her wings to show off their new lavender and magenta colors.

'Haven't you found love yet?' asked Slug, whose office was on the branch above Duck's.

'I write love letters every day,' said Cuckoo. 'They will attract someone.' She applied more lipstick, which looked a little odd on a big pointed beak.

'Are those yours?' asked Duck. 'The ones that say "I want you"?'

'Aren't they cool?' asked Cuckoo. 'I knew you'd groove on them.' She shook out her feather boa and wrapped it around herself.

'Groove?' said Goose. 'When did I last hear that?' He glanced at his pocket watch, as though to check the date of 'groove.'

'Isn't it cool?' Cuckoo fluffed her straggly feathers, her own and the boa's.

'Cool? How can old slang be cool?' asked Duck. 'By definition, slang is current.'

'I forget how old you are,' Cuckoo told Duck, shaking her feathered fan at him.

'You forget how old you are,' said Duck. 'You're no longer an adolescent.'

'I'm very young!' Cuckoo stamped her foot and shook her boa. Since her boa and fan were made of feathers, she created a swirl of colors—aqua, turquoise, coral, hot pink, lime green, and some not seen here.

'You were middle-aged when you got here, years ago,' said Goose, losing patience with her posing and affectations.

'I'm very young!' Cuckoo repeated.

'You're very cuckoo,' said Goose, walking away.

White Rabbit led Red Dean and Dragon Lady into the remains of Caedmon Hall. A window in the roof had been opened to create a door into the basement, all that was left of the three floors. The computers that usually filled basement offices were pushed into a corner of one room. One person seemed happy and dry, perhaps because he was more shade than substance, silvery white all over. 'That's Fox,' Goose told Alix. 'First he was made dean, then promoted to provost, then chancellor. Finally, last Friday, he was apotheosized.' Fox smiled in satisfaction.

Red Dean pointed into the corner where the computers were piled up. 'Get those computers out. Dry them off. They need to dry off.'

'Computers can't dry off enough to be used again,' said Dragon Lady.

'Of course they can. I wash my typewriter in the shower and dry it,' said Red Dean.

'Typewriters are much simpler than computers, and the old manual ones like yours have no wiring at all, that's why you can wash them off.' Dragon Lady glanced at Red Dean. 'Although I've never heard of anyone else doing that.'

'They should,' said Red Dean. 'What's all this about wiring?'

'Computers have wiring, lots of wires, and water creates shorts, Red Dean.'

'Turn one on so we can see,' Red Dean said, unconvinced. 'What's a few shorts anyway?'

Dragon Lady knew very little about electricity, but she did know this. 'Shorts are electric sparks that can cause someone to be electrocuted.' She hoped this wouldn't give

Red Dean ideas of creating little electric shock treatments. Anything was possible with Red Dean.

'Find someone to try it out,' said Red Dean. 'I won't throw away computers that can be dried and used.' She looked around, then up into the trees. 'Duck! Come use this computer!'

'She saw me!' cried Duck softly. Then, out loud, 'Can't, Red Dean, I don't use computers!' He ducked behind Goose.

'And you call yourself faculty!' Red Dean gasped. 'Learn to. Immediately!'

Duck whispered to Goose, 'As soon as she learns how.'

Red Dean was distracted by the sight of an art professor working at her easel. 'There's Flamingo. Fires, floods, blizzards, fiscal challenges, nothing bothers Flamingo. She just goes on painting the same crummy painting day after day.' Red Dean called out to Flamingo, 'Oh, a painting. I see you've got a nice new painting all started.' Then she turned to Dragon Lady and said in a lower voice, 'They appreciate my attention so much. That's one of the keys to my success with faculty.'

Dragon Lady waved a wing around Caedmon's ruined basement. 'I think this is going to get a whole lot worse before it gets any better.'

White Rabbit said, 'It is better. See how I've repaired Caedmon?' He sounded confident, but his paws shook and his eyes teared up. He lived in terror of Red Dean's wrath.

'Repaired! Repaired?' said Red Dean. 'Three floors are gone, with all the offices and homes that were in them. Now I'm told the computers are unusable.' She inhaled, grew purple, and glared at White Rabbit. 'And now you tell me you repaired Caedmon? You told everybody you had saved it.'

'I was in command,' said White Rabbit, shaking. 'I told the firefighters to save it.'

'It fell on me, remember?' said Red Dean. 'And it burned Dragon Lady.' She inhaled four times as she remembered being flattened in the crash of Caedmon. At least her three floors of records were safe in Boiling Point.

'I wasn't even there when it began,' said the trembling White Rabbit. 'And the firefighters were slow to respond when I called. The dispatcher explained that the fire chief was out of town, the assistant was working and not available, the fire station telephone was out of order and the fire horn was not working, which produced a complete void in the department for half an hour.'

Dragon Lady seemed to reignite. 'I was burned! You did not save the building from the fire!' She stood up taller than ever and flared her wings and nostrils and hair.

'I ordered it torn down to get the fire out,' said White Rabbit, his voice quavering. 'We got the fire out. There's a skill to being in command.' He held himself tightly so she couldn't see him trembling.

'And you don't have it,' said Dragon Lady. 'You pulled the building down!'

'The firefighters did that, to save it from fire!' But White Rabbit thought he was not going to win this debate if Red Dean and Dragon Lady were going to gang up on him.

Pigeon, Duck, and Goose were still watching from the trees. Pigeon said, 'The thing is, we've lost our offices and homes.' She was living in an old parachute bag hanging from a limb.

Goose said, 'All who prefer to view the current situation with increasing alarm, please signify by saying, "Aye!" ' He was somewhat alarmed himself, perched high in a tree for the first time in many years. He wanted to rise to the top, but not to a treetop.

Pigeon looked about. 'I daresay you're right about the view. I just never bothered to look out of the window.' She now looked around the campus.

'Doesn't she ever listen to what others are saying?' asked Goose, clinging to his branch with wings and big flat feet.

'She heard the word "view" but nothing else,' said Duck, regretting he wasn't a wood duck. He followed Goose farther out on a limb, grabbing at tiny branches to balance himself.

Goose saw that Cuckoo was lopsided on her branch. 'What's wrong with Cuckoo?'

'She does look slanted over,' agreed Duck. 'She has her up days and her down days. Today she seems to be tipped over.' His feet were wedged between the branches to steady him.

'She said nothing really happened to her, so she decided to become a character,' said Goose. His perch was precarious. How would he ever keep office hours?

'Well, her character matches her name,' said Duck as he wedged his desk into the fork of a branch. He was actually glad his computer was gone. The thought of an electric line running up the tree was too much.

Red Dean and Dragon Lady finished their tour of Caedmon Hole (its new name) and left for Boiling Point to review the success of the Lobster Quadrille. Red Dean was pleased with her lobsters. 'We've solved most of our problems. Boar is settled in the gazebo. Gila Monster has things under control. White Rabbit has a roof and thinks it's a building.'

'As long as he thinks that, you won't need to replace Caedmon,' commented Dragon Lady. He can have his virtual building, virtual command post, and virtual authority.

'My initial inclination was to wake the president up,' said Red Dean. 'Then you said, "Wait a minute. Why are we bothering him if there's nothing he needs to do?" '

'I remember,' said Dragon Lady. 'I stopped you just in time. You don't need to ask for funds to replace Caedmon Hall. We just needed to rename it Caedmon Hole. White Rabbit can pretend it's fine.'

'You were clever,' said Red Dean. 'When higher levels of command get involved in the decision-making, they always foul up.'

Dragon Lady said, 'I've had a message from Toad. He's called in an old friend of his to act as outside evaluator.' Since Toad's department was not located in Boiling Point, he could do many things differently because there was no one to see what he was doing.

'Of Toad's own department?' asked Red Dean. 'Even Boar doesn't go that far. Boar submits a list of his accomplishments. He has a consulting business, run from an apartment 150 miles away, and he contracts with one of his consultants to evaluate him. He pays well since he uses institutional funds to support his business contracts.'

'Toad wanted to be sure he'd get a good evaluation. He did. His friend wrote that Toad was brilliant, that the department was efficient, and that the only real problem was a person who thought Toad should work every day.' Dragon Lady despised Toad for his laziness but admired this scheme he had concocted to avoid working most days. She never got a day off.

'What did Toad do about this problem?' asked Red Dean, always anxious to solve problems of this type. She usually fired the problem.

'The person was singled out for criticism,' said Dragon Lady, glad to be back in Red Dean's good graces. She consulted a list of staff members who were afraid of Boar and Toad.

'So Toad practically wrote his own evaluation?' Red Dean was impressed. 'I did not think he could ever manipulate such a review.' She wished she'd thought of this herself, a painless review. She would never dismiss an appointee just because of a horrible evaluation; it would be to admit an error in appointing that person in the first place. It was much easier and much safer to stick with the appointee no matter how dismal the review.

'Oh, he could give lessons in surviving. Surviving by working half of each week,' said Dragon Lady. 'He beats us all at that, and I always thought Boar's scheme was the best—two incomes.' She knew that Boar's scheme was illegal, but she also knew he would get away with it.

'How does Toad manage that schedule?' Red Dean seemed more interested in Toad's short work week than in Boar's use of institutional funds to support his own business.

'Conferences. Meetings far away. He takes twice as long to reach each destination as everyone else. And twice as long to return.' Dragon Lady was surprised that Red Dean had not known this. Everyone in Toad's office complained about his three-day, often two-day weeks.

Red Dean seemed impressed. 'So he had himself evaluated by a friend. That's how he survived.' She knew it wasn't because of impressive work, for Toad was incompetent.

'He has one other advantage. His supervisor is Dean Dodo, who never wants to draw attention to himself or his subordinates.' Dragon Lady adjusted her scarves.

'Yes,' said Red Dean. 'Dodo reminds me of Janus. He worked to get power but cannot enjoy it. Janus can hardly sleep when he remembers that someone, somewhere, is doing something on his own.' That obsession to control distinguished Janus from Turkey, who complied automatically, while Janus calculated what his position would be after complying. Janus aimed for more power, but Turkey mainly wanted to protect his salary, grants, paid leaves, and his three labs. Turkey was much easier for her to terrorize.

Dragon Lady said, 'I overheard Dodo tell Toad: "Terrify subordinates, mind the upstairs and downstairs relationships, discipline oneself to avoid consistency, and you will become one of those rare managers who always profit from their employment." Avoid consistency. I like that.'

'I'd thank you, Dragon Lady, but yours is a thankless job,' said Red Dean. 'Are we finished with the quadrille?' She'd had a busy day, and there was much more to do. She would have her assistant Frog search the E-mail records to make sure everything was still there.

'I think you still need to remove a chair,' said Dragon Lady. 'Have you decided who has to go? Boar? White Rabbit? Gila Monster? Toad?'

'They're all too valuable to me,' said Red Dean. 'I've dismissed Counsellator.'

'He was very well liked by the students,' said Dragon Lady.

'Yesssssss.' Dragon Lady couldn't tell whether the hiss was a leak or a comment. Perhaps Red Dean's body was springing a leak. Dragon Lady saw a continuous wave traveling up through Red Dean's layers of dress, which looked like a partially collapsed tent.

'And the faculty,' said Dragon Lady, dreading having to explain this dismissal.

'Yesssss. What's your point?' Red Dean hissed again, and Dragon Lady knew it was a comment.

'And his staff. He raised morale there,' added Dragon Lady, wrapping her wings tightly around herself.

'Raised morale is fine and good for him but a problem for me,' said Red Dean. 'Raised morale means a more secure staff, not so jumpy.' Her side deflated a bit and hissed.

'You prefer them jumpy?'

'There's a quality of frogness that I find lacking in the world today,' said Red Dean.

'Your work is done now?' Dragon Lady wanted to relax before the next round of dismissals.

'For today,' said Red Dean. 'I'd like to gather them all and say, "Dearly beloved, we are gathered here again . . ."
—to arouse their curiosity, then spring it on them—"One more person has been eliminated from our community," and watch their faces freeze. It makes my day complete.'

'What's next, faculty trials?' asked Dragon Lady.

'Always educational for the community,' said Red Dean.

Alix found herself in another sculpture garden. She circled among the statues and saw a stork, two flamingos, two frogs, three rabbits, a Smoky the Bear, a skunk, three squirrels, a possum, and a Bambi. She decided they were probably monuments to members of the community, to departed staff members. She noticed that none of these were threatening characters, only harmless animals. She thought that the Boars and Gila Monsters had probably forced out the rabbits and squirrels and Bambi. It seemed that the deserving animals were the ones to go, leaving the bullies intact. She held Puppy to her chest tightly.

Chapter Eleven

Who Tarted the Sole?

E veryone was gathering in the old gym for the faculty trials. The building had been condemned years
ago, but there was no budget to tear it down. An
appropriate place to condemn people, the old gym was
filled with wrestling mats, exercise equipment, and office
furniture. Red Dean called it the Dispensation District and
had ordered her staff to arrange it to resemble a courtroom, with her chair at the judge's position. Red Dean
opened the faculty trials with the case against Otter.
'Summon Otter!' she said. 'Otter is charged with adding
pepper to the fish dish at our Picnic for the Institutional
Community.' It was soon obvious to Alix that Red Dean
was judge, jury, and prosecutor in this case. Red Dean
turned to Otter. 'You know how important community is

to all of us! How could you dare to ruin the sole? How dare you add pepper to the fish!'

Alix thought, How can she be both judge and prosecutor?

Otter replied, 'I didn't ruin it, I added flavor.' Otter looked at the audience, mostly faculty members, and saw several of them nod. Alix sat with Goose, Duck, Mad Hatter, and March Hare. Mad Hatter nodded vigorously, shaking her pink top hat. They were close enough to see the red veins in Red Dean's neck, but not close enough for her to hear their stage whispers.

'And what makes you think we need flavor?' demanded Red Dean, bouncing into the prosecutor's chair, her clothes and necklaces bouncing with her. Today her four necklaces included coral beads from Malaya, jade from Japan, seed diamonds from South Africa, and obsidian from Mexico. Another multicultural day.

'I thought the dish was flat,' said Otter. March Hare made a gesture of flattening something, as though she was making scones, or mudcakes.

'Flat? So now we're flat?' Red Dean gasped three times in quick succession, sending her tent dress fluttering. 'The evidence is mounting against you!' She had a lingering fear of flatness.

'What evidence?' asked Goose under his breath. 'This is simply amazing! Red Dean's taken ordinary behavior and through threats and exaggeration turned it into a charge of misbehavior!' But Because Goose was in the audience, he could not testify officially. No one could. Otter had been summoned but had not been told what the charges were, so no defense was planned or allowed.

Otter said, 'You're not flat. You're round as a balloon.' Otter knew that Red Dean always redefined the argument if she could, and now Red Dean had twisted the charge from peppering the fish to insulting herself, and from fish flavor to dean shape.

Red Dean banged her gavel. 'Otter admits guilt. Dismiss her from the institution.'

'And jury, too?' said Alix out loud.

Duck, watching from the audience, said, 'Where's the defense attorney? Even Packrat had a defense attorney when he was dismissed for having a messy desk.'

'So did Robin when Red Dean tried her for having six comma faults in her last grant proposal,' added Goose. 'She's now chair of her department somewhere else.'

Pigeon replied, 'You'll see a defense attorney at the next trial. They can't be everywhere.' Even from the sidelines, out of Red Dean's hearing, Pigeon automatically defended the decrees.

Duck said, 'Otter's always been an effective teacher. Doesn't that count?'

Red Dean shouted, 'We can't have any interruptions from the audience. Otter's pepper made tempers hot. That's cause for dismissal.' To the guards she ordered, 'Remove Otter.' The guards were four owls, who promptly surrounded Otter and escorted her outside, where she was stripped of her faculty identity card, her keys, and her E-mail address.

Watching the owls, Goose commented, 'There's such a thing as being too damned owlish.' He was sitting on a torn couch, far away from Red Dean's seat, so she didn't hear him.

As many of the spectators objected loudly to the verdict, the bailiff, Turkey Lurkey, restored order: 'Hear ye, hear ye, hear her, hear me, hear who, here where, here why. . .' At first no one heard him because his contact lenses were upside down and so was his head. Then, after the noise had abated, Turkey Lurkey turned to Red Dean. 'The next case, your deaconry, concerns these five faculty who kicked students.' He made a kicking motion five times, a difficult deed indeed with an upside-down head.

Red Dean said, 'I'll separate the cases. What is the first case?' She now sat in the judge's seat because she would no longer act as both judge and prosecutor. Janus would prosecute—that is, Janus's round frown face would. The other face had swiveled to the back and checked out.

Janus JekyllHyde said, 'The first case concerns Musk-rat. Twenty-three students have accused Muskrat of kicking them. All twenty-three signed the complaint against him. I sent the report to you on E-mail.'

'Did the kicks hurt?' asked Red Dean, forgetting that kicks were strictly forbidden.

'The students said so,' said Janus JekyllHyde. 'Some said he also spit on them.'

Red Dean decided to ignore the spitting. 'Where did these kicks occur?' she asked.

'Mostly in Windy Hole, in the corridors. He lured the students down the dark corridors, then tripped them and kicked them while they were down.' Both of Janus's faces had seen the tangle of kicked students lying on the floor of the corridor, and his lean and sleepy face cried, while the round frowning face ordered the students to stop lying about.

'In the dark corridors?' asked Red Dean. 'Did any witnesses come forward?' She had no time to hear a bunch of witnesses; she had several more verdicts to issue.

'The only witnesses are other victims. They were with Muskrat after class.'

'They are biased,' said Red Dean. 'Where is the defense?' Hearing objections from the audience, she banged her gavel hard, causing herself to bounce into the air.

'I am the defense,' said Janus JekyllHyde's mild face. 'There are no unbiased witnesses.' His control face smiled in anticipation of victory.

'We certainly can't prosecute someone because in a moment of emotion he made a mistake,' said Red Dean. 'Case dismissed. Call the next case.' She was feeling quite efficient—that was a complicated case, and she had finished it quickly to everyone's satisfaction. Everyone who mattered, that is. She would have the whole afternoon free to reread the week's E-mail again.

Alix could hardly believe what she was hearing. 'Why do these cases move so fast?' she asked Duck. 'Red Dean hardly listens to the case before deciding it.'

'Well, that's because she has already decided them. We're here only to hear her decisions. They're logged on, packaged up, and ready to apply.'

As Janus came forward, Goose said, 'Now we'll hear from Professor Janus JekyllHyde, whose weak scholarship is balanced by his mighty tenure.'

'Your deaconry,' said the prosecutor Janus JekylHyde, 'the next case is more serious. Beaver is accused of befriending a student, then kicking her when she wasn't looking.' Janus frowned as usual, but Alix saw something of a smile beneath his mustache. She'd never seen him smile before.

'Befriending, you say?' Red Dean inhaled. 'Did he invite her to his house?' Red Dean looked at the audience to direct their attention to this complicated case. She felt that Beaver was fair, compassionate, and intelligent, but that most of the faculty perceived him as biased, callous, and dumb. Her necklaces jangled as she inhaled again.

'Yes, many times, and many other students as well.' Janus looked approvingly at Beaver, knowing that he would have Beaver's undying loyalty. Beaver looked back and smirked, knowing he had Red Dean's undying approval. After all, he fed more students than she did, so he was more communal.

'Did they eat meals at his house?' asked Red Dean, now glowing fuchsia with approval.

'Many meals, on a regular basis,' said Janus Jekyll-Hyde. His defense face, the mild and sleepy one, was doing all the work in this case, and it smiled back at Beaver.

'Then he was extending hospitality. He was helping create a sense of community. That's what we're all about here, a wonderful community.' Red Dean was now pulsing from fuchsia to pink to maroon to lavender with satisfaction. 'He's eminently sane, and a credit to our community.'

'He's very community-oriented.' Janus knew that he only had to respond correctly, that the case was already settled in Red Dean's mind. Someday, he thought, if he played his cards right, he would be in a position to dish out decisions. He knew he could dish and deal with the best of them.

'I've always thought so,' said Red Dean. 'Case dismissed.'

Mad Hatter and March Hare were watching with unsurprised horror from their perch on a rolled-up wrestling mat. 'We have continuous tea parties! We entertain the community! She's using political criteria when she says Beaver is "eminently sane" and we're mad!' said Mad Hatter. 'Another one for my Atrocity File!'

'Maybe we should kick students,' said March Hare. 'Then we'll see if she calls us "eminently sane," as she called Beaver. Anything goes for him!'

'He goes right into my Atrocity File!' cried Mad Hatter, adjusting her black pith helmet, which she always wore to these trials. She felt secure from verbal and actual brickbats that way.

Red Dean could not hear the conversation among the spectators. Neither could Janus JekyllHyde, who said to her, 'The next three cases are even more serious. We have kept the names secret to protect the participants.'

Mad Hatter asked, 'Which names? The victims or the accused?'

'Both! All the names, victims and accused, especially the accused,' whispered Duck.

'Red Dean says they're "eminently sane," too,' cried March Hare, so upset she spilled the tea on her gloves and skirt.

Alix thought, Aren't they all mad, in a larger sense? She at last understood why Mad Hatter and March Hare refused to participate in the races, the croquet match, the power struggles. She understood the tea parties, the tea-cart, the dresses, the hats. 'So that's why you wear those party dresses—they're bizarre.'

'Bizarre situations call for bizarre acts!' Mad Hatter fluffed her bazaar clothes from Algeria and rattled her six Mexican bracelets.

'That's our motto,' exclaimed March Hare. 'Bizarre situations call for bizarre acts!'

Goose whispered furiously to himself, 'Time to recite, time to recite.'

'What!' Mad Hatter, whose hearing was wonderfully acute, exclaimed again and again, 'What! What!'

March Hare, whose hearing, alas, had much declined of late, looked amazed at her friend. 'What what?' she asked. But Mad Hatter was already bounding toward Goose. March Hare followed.

'Goose,' said Mad Hatter, 'will recite.'

'Here? Now?' March Hare gasped. Alix joined them.

'Goose will recite,' she told Alix.

'What?' Alix asked, pleased, for she loved to hear poetry, and she had been told how marvelously Goose recited.

March Hare and Mad Hatter said as one, ' "The Trial of Blackbeetle." '

A hush fell over that corner of the room, a hush unheard by Red Dean, who went on trying, rapt with well-being and power. Other creatures sidled over quietly, surrounding Goose on his sofa. They stood expectantly. Goose seemed to become something or someone else before their eyes, something older, larger. His brows furrowed, his feathers rose, until he seemed twice his size. And his dark yellow eyes lost their glow. They glazed over as if he were struck blind. Alix was impressed. She could have sworn she heard, coming from somewhere far, far away, the sounds of a stringed instrument, a lute, perhaps, but played in a scale she had never heard before.

After several minutes of a silence broken only by this imaginary music, Goose began to speak:

> I sing of Blackbeetle the Brave, Heroine of our Halls.
> Singly she stood against Horror, seizing the Dark Dean,
> Fastening her mighty Fangs upon his Darkness.
> He flailing, they fell many leagues, till at last
> They descended to the depths of the River of Darkness
> Beneath Windy Hole and there battled days on end, they.
> Dark Dean with his terrible spells cursed and condemned
> Blackbeetle trapped forever in this place of Despair.
> Did she not free her fangs, but she would not waver,
> Not she. She clung to him harder, fearless in the face
> Of the changes he made: bellowing bear, lion outraged,
> Murderous Angel, Beast of the Deep. Nor would she be
> Shaken by strangeness: Shower of stinging bees,
> Briar bushes, terrible winds. Through all these shapes
> She stayed fast, steeling her heart against fear.
> Beyond Time, they wrestled in Darkness, age on age,
> Until the Dark Dean cried, "Enough! I give what you will."
> Then, for the first time, Blackbeetle spoke: "Freedom," she said.
> Dark Dean, enraged, wrestled on in horrible shapes,
> Age on age again: ramping badger, smooth politician,
> Committee chair, royal regent, dragons of air. Still
> Blackbeetle clung, strong in her passion for Freedom.

During the last six verses, Alix had heard another voice, at first faint, then growing intense. 'What's that? What's that?' the voice was asking. Red Dean had emerged sufficiently from her stupor of self-satisfaction to be aware of the knot of figures surrounding Goose and the cadence of his reciting. Finally, Alix heard her clearly. 'What are you reciting?' Red Dean bellowed. 'A forbidden poem?!' Goose's trance dropped from him. March Hare and Mad Hatter assumed their guises again. 'Nothing. Oh, nothing!' both giggled in unison.

'It had better be!' bellowed Red Dean. 'Back to your places!'

Alix returned with March Hare and Mad Hatter to their seats. Alix whispered to March Hare, 'What a strange poem. What does it mean?'

'It's an allegory, my dear,' March Hare replied. 'I will explain later.'

Still unable to hear the spectators, Red Dean asked Janus, 'These three faculty also kicked students? I find it hard to understand why anyone would kick students when they know that we forbid it. The penalties are very severe when someone is found guilty. Why would anyone do it, knowing the penalties? You say all three kicked students?'

'Undoubtedly,' said Janus JekyllHyde. 'Everyone agrees about that. All the kickers and all the kickees.'

'Have the victims been interviewed?' Red Dean firmly believed in debriefing victims.

'Yes,' said Janus JekyllHyde. 'As prosecuting officer, I interviewed them many times.'

'Have they been told that we are doing everything possible to investigate their cases?' She just as firmly believed in briefing them with the correct information.

'Yes, your deaconry. As attorney for the defense, I cross-examined them thoroughly.'

'Good. This has been an exquisite investigation!' cried Red Dean. 'You are someone who knows right from wrong.'

Janus JekyllHyde said, 'Everyone is aware of the penalties for kicking.'

'And everyone is aware that no penalties are ever enforced,' whispered Mad Hatter to Alix.

'Because restrictions against kicking have not been effective, total abstinence is probably the best practical solution to the problem,' said Red Dean. She bounced a little in her chair. 'Send a general E-mail to all the faculty. Kicking is strictly forbidden.'

Alix was dumbfounded. 'So the "solution" is the same as the "restriction"?'

'Exactly!' said Mad Hatter. 'A perfect circle of absurdity!'

'Then these cases are over?' asked Janus.

'These three cases are over,' Red Dean said. 'We've protected confidentiality; that's the most important thing. Wonderful investigation!'

Goose whispered, 'The most important thing was protecting the accused; that's obvious.'

Goose, Duck, Alix, Mad Hatter, and March Hare watched the celebration at the end of the trials. Red Dean, Janus JekyllHyde, and all the defendants were planning to leave soon for Beaver's home. He had a meal waiting for them, cooked by his new student friends.

'Things continue to continue,' commented Mad Hatter. 'Red Dean decides, then things continue.'

As she was leaving, Red Dean said, 'Those were the most orderly trials I've seen here.'

'She would think so,' said Goose. 'She's coerced both the victims and the accused into obedience.'

Duck commented, 'I wouldn't mind a little disorder in court now and then. It would break the cursed monotony. Red Dean has prepackaged every case. Prejudged, prepackaged, predictated. She might as well send out the verdicts through E-mail, like the other directives.'

'Why didn't Janus's second face object to the trials?' asked Alix.

'He wants to speak out,' said Goose, 'but he hasn't found the proper forum.'

As Red Dean and her cronies left the meeting room, Alix thought of her adventures since arriving at the institution. At times she had been frightened: she'd been lost in Windy Hole and Mazin Grates, lost her clothes, ID, and backpack, and almost her life in Caedmon Hall. At other times she was not frightened but amused: by the chaos of the mud races, the croquet match, and the tea party. At the

time, she had only seen the chaos, and she hadn't understood who was in charge. Now she knew it was Red Dean
and her three floors of E-mail records. Looking back at all
of those experiences, and now the trials, it seemed to her
that Red Dean consistently punished those who were
relaxed, agreeable, and fundamentally lighthearted and
rewarded the tense, the venous, and the mean.

'Speaking of prepackaging,' said Mad Hatter, 'isn't it
time for the faculty search committees? There's not much
time left this summer for all the searches. Have they decided whom they're going to hire?'

'Most of the searching is done,' said Duck. 'Psychometrics gave tenure to their temporary staff member.'
Duck and Goose invited Alix to join them in a walk, where
they could speak openly.

'Gave? No training?' asked Goose. 'No search?' He
gestured toward the barns and they headed in that direction. Mad Hatter and March Hare now caught up with
them, again riding their teacart. Mad Hatter was wearing
an emerald green garden-party dress with a flared skirt,
green spike heels, and an extravagantly brimmed green
straw hat with flowers on the brim. March Hare's leisure
suit matched green for green, making a vista of green flowing down the grassy green slope.

'It wasn't necessary. She resembled the retiring member so much she didn't need any treatment. You have to
give it to those Psychos. They know how to work the system,' said Duck.

'How about Hysterics?' asked Mad Hatter. 'Did they
convert their new person into tenure?' Mad Hatter offered
everyone some appetizers. Only Duck declined, having
eaten the orchids in the courtroom, assuming they were
hors d'oeuvres.

Goose said, 'They may have to search, but they have
a plan. Their search will find Petunia.' Mad Hatter meanwhile searched for her teapot.

'Petunia? The person already teaching?' asked Mad Hatter, giving a little shudder at the memory of Petunia. She was afraid of Petunia's expression of undisguised hostility, even when Petunia tried to hide it with an expression of amused contempt. She ate two cookies and drank a cup of tea to calm herself.

'Yes, the plan is infallible. They'll find Petunia.' Goose had a friend in Hysterics who had spilled the plan by accident.

'And the search in Humane Etudes?' asked Mad Hatter. 'Don't they also have a temporary person they can convert into permanent?'

'That was the plan,' said Duck. 'Red Dean told everyone it was all arranged, but you know the old saying, "A verbal agreement isn't worth the paper it is printed on." Something fell through.'

'Any other dismissals?' asked Goose. 'Or is it only Otter?'

Duck said, 'Spangles decided not to convert their temporary person to permanent, so their search specifically excludes her. She's out. She was dismissed yesterday.'

'Wow!' said March Hare. 'Spangles has really got it upstairs! They thought of a foolproof method of dismissing someone, even without a trial.'

They turned back after their walk to the barn, since the sheep were in the meadow and the cow was in the corn, and they walked towards the student center. All of the students were still at the picnic, but Henny Penny was in the middle of a presentation. She was in the lobby with an easel containing a poster. The poster showed several converging lines leading down at the right side. She pointed at the intersection of the lines as she told Pigeon, Cuckoo, Crab, Slug, and Drone, 'And so, extrapolating from the best figures available, we see that current trends, unless dramatically reversed, will inevitably lead to a situation in which the sky will fall.' She looked at each of them. 'I told you, they're trying to finish us off!'

Chapter Twelve

Alix's Evidence

Alix went with Goose, Drone, Slug, Mad Hatter, and March Hare to the student lounge. She liked the weird underwater motif on the walls, all the tropical fish, crabs, shrimp, manta rays, eels, and coral. Sitting down next to Slug, she asked him if the faculty trials were always that trying. 'You missed a real show last year,' he said. 'Bob Vivant was tried for ill-treating prawns. He was cooking them on a hot plate, so Red Dean charged him with cruelty to his dinner.'

'Were you here the year that Bunny was tried for throwing avocado pits at the prowlers in his back yard?'

Mad Hatter asked Slug. 'Or the year that April Hare ate with the wrong fork? They're gone now.'

'So's Snake,' said Slug. 'Shaped like an apostrophe, but he could never use them effectively. He's gone, first to a treatment center, then dismissed permanently.'

'Unlimited power,' said Drone, 'that's the problem. Do you remember when she found Squirrel nesting in the old upright piano in here? She played the Lost Chord, and Squirrel shot straight out of the top of the piano, and we've never seen her again.'

'We didn't even have a trial,' said Duck, who had come in just in time to hear the last two stories. 'The person I miss is Gopher, who was dismissed for wearing dresses. As straight as the Kansas Interstate, he just wanted to wear dresses once in a while, but Red Dean dismissed him for failing to have a proper professional appearance.'

'I thought he looked better than she did, and they had some of the same dresses,' said Slug, remembering in particular a bright yellow party dress with beautiful lace designs.

'Do you remember the seven-layer Jello mold I made last year?' asked March Hare. 'I was so careful to keep the layers from bleeding into each other, but when I served it the colors were not arranged in the same order as a rainbow, so Red Dean said I was insubordinate. How could anyone maintain self-respect by playing politics with Red Dean? Look what it has done to Turkey Lurkey and Pigeon and Janus JekyllHyde. They never stopped running scared.' Better to choose as she and Mad Hatter had chosen, she told Alix, 'We considered other options. Mad Hatter favored nihilism, I opted for militancy, we compromised on anarchism with a bit of anachronism thrown in.'

'The long dresses! The Gibson girl hats! The veils! The white gloves!' Alix cried.

'Exactly. Now you see.'

Alix thought of the assembly, when she heard about the best dorms and the best students and the best food.

And she thought of the high-minded goals expressed by the dean: love, fairness, autonomy, freedom, and community. The love and community she had seen was from Slug, Drone, Duck, Goose, Mad Hatter, and March Hare, faculty members who avoided Red Dean. Those close to Red Dean, like Turkey Lurkey and Janus, shared her autocratic absolutism. Those who hoped for more power, like Dragon Lady, Caterpillar, and Preying Praying Mantis, practiced absolutism to impress Red Dean. Alix was afraid of all of them and knew that Red Dean's professions of love, freedom, autonomy, and community were as empty as she herself was.

Red Dean's sense of community drove her to dismiss Otter to protect the community—from what? From pepper? From hot tempers? What about the other hot tempers? Alix wondered who might be the next to go, Mad Hatter, or March Hare, or Slug, or Goose?

White Rabbit and Ostrich walked in together. White Rabbit was shaking and muttering to himself. 'They're against me; this time I can feel it.'

'You're paranoid,' said Ostrich. 'Who do you think is against you?' As usual, Ostrich's role was to calm frightened and nervous faculty.

'Red Dean, Dragon Lady, Turkey Lurkey, Janus Jekyll-Hyde,' said White Rabbit. 'They think I failed to save Caedmon Hall.'

'I wish we could all go back in time,' said Ostrich. 'If all of this had just never happened.' He looked at White Rabbit. 'They say time heals all wounds.'

'I hope time wounds all heels,' said White Rabbit. He sat close to Ostrich, ready to hide behind him if Red Dean or Dragon Lady came in, and trembled like a rabbit.

Turkey Lurkey approached with Pigeon. 'Janus is unfit to be a prosecutor,' he said. 'He should have suppressed all of the cases, totally suppressed them before they could hurt the community.' Turkey considered himself an expert on prosecutors. Besides, his lenses were upright today, for the first time in months.

'All of them?' asked Pigeon. She glanced at Duck and Goose because she knew they had odd fixations about Janus; they thought he was lawyerly but not legal.

'All of the kicking cases,' said Turkey Lurkey. 'We can't let students tell us what to do about faculty. Just because they said something happened doesn't mean it did happen.' He ordered a bowl of popcorn.

'You're absolutely right about that,' said White Rabbit. 'Students can't tell us what to do. Usually they are wrong about everything.

'Janus wants Red Dean's position,' said Pigeon, who regarded her role as maker of sense.

'He's unfit for the deaconry,' said Turkey Lurkey. 'He has two opinions about everything, and his faces argue more often than not. Red Dean, on the other hand, has one consistent opinion.' Turkey also thought himself an expert on deanly affairs.

'Has the faculty ever been polled as to their choice of dean?' asked Alix.

'I'm an expert on polling,' said Turkey Lurkey, 'and the latest research on polls has turned up something interesting. People will tell you any old thing that pops into their heads.'

'Red Dean seems to be too tired to go on,' said Goose. 'Before, all that heat inside kept her going. Now she's losing air. Or maybe heat. Anyway, she's drooping, that's for sure.'

'Hot air! That's all she is! Hot air!' said Mad Hatter, forgetting for a moment that Turkey was nearby, and that he carried reports of faculty conversations to Red Dean and carried grant money back. Yet another area of expertise, carrying tales and money!

'Fifty-six years with the wrong dean!' said Goose, too enraged to care who heard him.

'My goodness, I've got half a mind to put you on tape,' said Turkey Lurkey, taking out his tape recorder. He always carried a tiny recorder to capture any brilliant ideas he might suddenly have.

'What can Red Dean be thinking?' said Ostrich. 'We have a policy against kicking students, and severe penalties.' Ostrich assumed a severe expression.

'Who decides which policies to emphasize?' asked Duck. 'Who decides that kicking is okay?' Duck hoped that for once Ostrich would overrule Red Dean.

'Why is adding pepper worse than kicking students?' asked Goose, pursuing Duck's point.

'Red Dean runs a tight ship,' said Ostrich, seeming to forget that he was the admiral and Red Dean merely the commander of the ship.

'It's not a good idea to sound like you're riding a loose horse and about to go down with the ship,' said White Rabbit. Everyone stopped talking and stared at him.

'And they call you mad, ' Alix said to Mad Hatter. 'Does he mean "tight ship"?'

'Red Dean is preventing anarchy,' said Pigeon, 'so she has to run a tight ship.'

'Yeah, right. Anarchy,' said Mad Hatter. 'Hot pepper.' Turning away from the group, she sang a song that had just come into her head.

> Twinkle, twinkle, little dean,
> How I wonder why you're mean,
> Up above the school so high,
> Like a pisspot in the sky.

Preying Praying Mantis in a nearby room began addressing Dragon Lady, Red Dean, and Janus JekylHyde, so Alix and Ostrich joined the group. Preying Praying Mantis was giving a presentation: 'How many times have you wanted to pray at meetings but didn't? Or do you say the same prayer over and over until it begins to lose its meaning? The Prayer Toaster that I have developed encourages originality and regular prayer by your colleagues. Push the lever on the toaster and up pops a scripture verse and table prayer on a cardboard slice that looks like a piece of toast. I've written thirty different prayers.'

'I like it,' said Red Dean, always eager to promote cohesion and camaraderie in the community.

'The prayers are included, you say?' asked Ostrich.

'I've written each one,' said Preying Praying Mantis proudly.

Dragon Lady said, 'I'm sending out departmental requisitions this week. Hysterics has ordered leg irons, medieval axes, commando bayonets, pepper gas, and Gypsy daggers. I'll insert the Prayer Toaster in the order. How many do we need?'

'One for each faculty position,' said Red Dean. She leaned back in her chair. She *was* drooping. Before, she had been too round to lean back at all.

'Position? Not person?' asked Dragon Lady, leaning forward to be sure she heard.

'Each position. They'll leave them here when they leave the institution,' said Red Dean, smiling at the thought of improving faculty morale and morals in one order.

'Do you expect many to leave?' asked Ostrich, still a bit surprised at the dismissal of Otter and Counsellator.

'Not on their own. They're too passive,' said Red Dean. 'They're too dependent on my guidance. Many of them are as innocent as the new students, so I mother them as much as I can.'

'Most of them like it here anyway,' said Ostrich.

'Like! Like? They like it here? They can't just like it. They have to love it!' Red Dean inhaled quickly three times to replace her breath.

'Hysterics sent in one more order. It says they want two hundred crates of dinosaur bones unearthed in the Gobi last year,' said Dragon Lady.

'That sounds as if the dinosaur bones were discovered already packed in crates,' said Mantis.

'Hysterics wants them as they are, that's all I know,' said Dragon Lady, holding a note from Hysterics.

'Add the crates if that will make them happy.' Red Dean relaxed and expanded. Soon, everyone would be praying—and she would pick the prayers. At last, community on campus!

'Now we're done,' said Ostrich. 'We can all go back to our offices and departments and pretend we've been busy.'

Caterpillar had been busy, back in his office. Alix was summoned to meet with him at the Admissions Office in Boiling Point. Feeling grateful not to have to go through Mazin Grates again, she immediately hurried over to keep the appointment. Students who had fulfilled some of their General Requirements in the croquet match were collecting their Perspectives. Janus JekyllHyde was taking care of those students. Caterpillar had kept the appointment this time, so Alix sat near his desk.

'Who are youuuuuu?' he asked her, blowing blue smoke rings again.

'Alix,' she answered, as usual, wondering if he would ever remember who she was.

'I need to see your ID card,' said Caterpillar, blowing blue smoke around the room.

Trying not to breathe more than necessary, Alix said, 'My ID card washed away in the flood. All the ink washed off, so now it's blank.'

'But you need an ID to show who you are,' puffed Caterpillar.

'No,' said Alix, 'I don't. I know exactly who I am. Yesterday I didn't, but so many things have happened that I'm a different person, and I want to create my own major.'

'Well, well,' said Caterpillar, 'aren't you the little know-it-all?'

'No,' said Alix, 'but I do know who I am.' As she reached for the forms, she heard a loud hissing, then a

woosh from above and behind her. Four gold multicultural necklaces fell to the floor, then a large gray dress with
pink flowers. Alix recognized Red Dean's dress and necklaces and looked around to see where Red Dean was, but
she wasn't around.

'Red Dean's gone!' shouted Janus. 'She blew away!'

'Nonsense,' said Caterpillar. 'No one blows away.'

'She sprung a leak, began hissing more and more, and
vanished,' insisted Janus. 'She had nothing inside but air
—no substance, no skeleton, no insides, nothing. She was
hollow through and through.'

Hearing this, Alix remembered the croquet match, the
crying students, those with swollen heads, those pounded
for not fitting in the hoops, those who ran away. There was
nothing left of Red Dean. She thought about the confusing requirements represented by the hoops.

Caterpillar said, 'I'll let you create your own major, as
you asked. Just fill out these forms.'

'No, I now know what I want,' said Alix, 'and it isn't
here.'

Eleanor nudged Alix. 'How long have you been sleeping?'

'Sleeping! So all that was a dream! It seemed like days,'
replied Alix. 'I dreamed I was in Wonderland, only it was
different, with Laurel and Hardy, Mae West, the Marx
Brothers, and some characters seemed like Pogo. It seemed
to be this college, but there was so much internal politics
involved, things I've never hear of.'

'You heard a lot of conversation from faculty members
as you slept. It must have inspired you,' said Eleanor. 'Welcome back!'

'In my dream the dean was like the Red Queen, trying
to get rid of people, only instead of "off with their heads!"
she wanted to fire everyone who didn't listen to her. She
had a croquet game, just like the Red Queen, and caucus

races, and assistants to scare people. It was a fantastic dream.'

'Maybe you should write it down so you won't forget it,' said Eleanor. 'Did it turn you off this college?'

'Not really, I don't turn off that easily, but I did see a lot of scary people, and I think I learned something. There's nothing so scary as allowing yourself to become scared of a person who threatens you. In my dream a lot of adults were too scared to act as themselves—they had to conform to rules and behavior.'

'So your dream taught you something?' asked Eleanor.

'Yes, to be sure of who I am, just like Alice.'

Jeanne Purdy teaches Humanities and Women's Studies courses at the University of Minnesota, Morris, and has always been inspired by *Alice inWonderland*.